Lost in the Wilderness

By R. E. Toresen

Photos by Marielle Andersson Gueye
Translated by Osa K. Bondhus

© Stabenfeldt 2006
© Photos: Marielle Andersson Gueye
© Photos of bears and wolf: Thony Kumral/Bildmejeriet
Translator: Osa K. Bondhus
Repro: Bryne Offset A/S
Printed in Italy, 2006
Editor: Bobbie Chase

ISBN: 1-933343-39-7

Stabenfeldt, Inc.
457 North Main Street
Danbury, CT 06811
www.pony.us

We would like to thank Anna at Söderåsens Turridning (www.turridning.se) in Helsingborg, Sweden, for all her help and for letting us use her Haflinger horses Mari, Dali, Annabel, Affe, Bella and Ronja, and Söderåsens Forsgård (www.soderasensforsgard.se) for letting us use their farm and house. We would also thank Emilie, Sofie, Paulina, Pia and Marie for being such excellent models.

Lost in the Wilderness

By R. E. Toresen

The main characters:

Alicia

Suzanne

Lily

Alicia's mother

Alicia's father

Gail

Jasper

Silas

Tofu

Chapter 1

I was standing in Roofus's stall with my face buried in his nice, warm coat. The tears, which I had managed to hold back on my way to the stable, now ran freely, drenching his neck. But he didn't seem to mind or care the slightest about my unusual behavior. He just stood there unaffected, his usual self, snatching straws of hay that he munched on with a steady, grinding motion. The familiar sounds and smells inside the stable usually made me happy, but not today.

"Oh, Roofus," I gasped. "What would I do without you? Everything is just terrible! You're the only one who loves me!"

I knew perfectly well that this was not true, but that's how I felt; neglected, abandoned and unwanted. My knees trembled because I had biked so hard. Never had I made it to the stable faster than I had today. After the detestable phone call, which had ruined everything, I had only one thought in my head: Roofus! I wanted Roofus! He was the only one who understood me. And he was the only one who could comfort me now. Roofus, my beautiful Haflinger [ho]rse, always made me feel welcome and wanted.

I lifted my head and looked at him through a veil of tears. [He] was the best friend a girl could have. And he was mine! [A] safe haven in an unsafe world," Grandma liked to say [ab]out him. She might as well have said the same thing [ab]out herself. Grandma has been the only stable [th]ing in my whole life for as long as I can [re]member. She lives in the same house [as] my parents and I, and works out of a home office as a freelance translator. Grandma takes care of me when my mom and dad are gone on work related trips, which they take constantly. And when they're home, they're so busy anyway; they don't have much time for me then, either. They keep saying that the next time they come home we'll do something fun together, but their promises rarely come to anything. Something always gets in the way, something that's more important.

"I know Grandma says that they love me," I sniffed as I wiped my eyes with my sleeve, "but it sure doesn't feel like it. Not right now, anyway." I had looked forward to this vacation so much, and now it was off.

Roofus tilted his head as he looked at me. His dark eyes seemed to ask, almost with reproach, "Are you saying you were looking forward to going somewhere without me?"

Of course, I knew he didn't think like that at all, but I still felt guilty.

"Of course I wasn't looking forward to leaving you," I said, stroking him across the soft muzzle. He sniffed at my hand and snorted when he didn't find any treats. In my haste to get out of the house I had totally forgotten to bring him some carrots, as I usually did.

"I'm sorry, I don't have anything for you today," I said and scratched his forehead. He loves that. He closed his eyes halfway, showing every sign of enjoying it, and hence possibly considering forgiving me for not bringing him treats.

"I'll make it up to you tomorrow by giving you twice the amount of carrots then," I said softly. In spite of my fresh

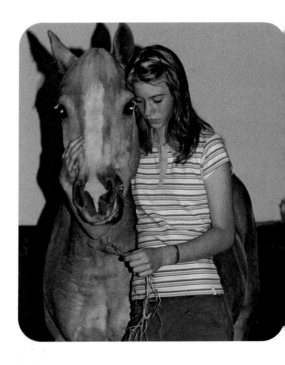

disappointment, I felt a wave of gratitude at the thought of being the owner of this wonderful horse. "I hope you know how much I would have missed you every day."

It was true. But even so, I had been extremely excited about our vacation plans. Two whole weeks on a beautiful Caribbean island, just Mom, Dad and me. The few times in my life that I had spent time alone with my parents we always had a great time together, and in those moments I was always convinced that nobody could have better and nicer parents than I had.

But then, only one day before we were supposed to leave, came that phone call which erased all our plans. I felt a knot in my stomach as I thought about it. We were eating breakfast when it happened. Dad was, as usual, sitting at the table with a cup of coffee in one hand and his favorite pen in the other. A notebook lay on the table, open and ready for another idea that might turn into his next book.

My dad is a writer who specializes in travel books about exciting and exotic places. He doesn't call himself a writer, though. He says he's simply an explorer who has no choice but to write about the places he goes in order to make a living. I don't know if it's true, or if it's just something he says for fun. At least he writes really well, according to the critics. I'm ashamed to admit that I have never read any of his books. I'm not sure why. Maybe it's because in a way I see them as my enemies, or rivals that take Dad away from me. And they take my mom away as well. She's a photographer, and always goes with Dad. She's the one who takes all the pictures for his books. The two of them are completely hooked on adventures, and if they come across a rare animal or bird on one of their trips, they can be ecstatic for weeks afterwards. Last time they were out exploring, somewhere in the Amazon area, they came across a bird species that had been widely believed to be extinct for a long time. Dad was so proud you'd think he'd hatched those stupid birds himself. Personally I think they should have left them alone. Now the poor birds have to cope with a bunch of scientists streaming to the jungle to study them since Dad's discovery became known. But when I said this to Dad, he just laughed at me.

"Maybe you should write a travel book about the island where you'll be staying on your vacation," Grandma suggested to him the other day. "Then you can stay home afterwards and write in peace and quiet."

Dad had merely snorted at her. "There're enough books already about that tourist mill," he said. "It's a bunch of beaches and palm trees, and no excitement at all. No, I'm thinking about something much better, a wilderness where no tourist has set foot yet. Actually I have something in the works, and I'm hoping it pans out."

"But first we'll have a wonderful, relaxing vacation," interrupted Mom with a smile toward me." I smiled back at her, feeling incredibly excited about the upcoming trip.

That's when the phone rang. I've seen it on TV shows, how people stiffen when the phone rings, as if they know beforehand that something unpleasant is about to happen. I had no such premonition. If I had had the slightest inkling what was about to happen, I would probably have thrown the phone right out the window. But as it was, I just walked over to the phone, picked up the receiver and said, "Hello." I figured it was one of my friends, calling to say goodbye. But the voice on the other end introduced himself as Mr. Henderson, and asked for my dad. There were still no warning bells in my head. The name didn't mean anything to me. I gave the phone to my dad and heard him say his name. Then he listened quietly for a while before he said, "I'm surprised to hear from you so soon. So everything is working out? Of course, I understand. And you think there really is something to those rumors? I see... When ..."

I saw his face change suddenly while he listened to the answer. The smile disappeared, and he glanced over at me. I wondered why. Could it be somebody calling to complain about me? I tried to remember if Roofus and I had been riding somewhere we weren't supposed to or something, but I couldn't think of anything. Not since that time when Roofus

had been spooked by a car horn honking at us. He ran right into old Mr. Anderson's yard, stepping on some flowers in the flurry. Mr. Anderson wasn't very happy about it! But that was a long time ago... I couldn't help chuckling at the thought.

Then I returned to the present. Dad hung up the phone, and was looking at me again. His facial expression showed very clearly that he was about to say something he knew I wasn't going to like...

"How could he?" I leaned into Roofus as I felt the tears welling up again. "He canceled our vacation, just because some dork arranged a wilderness expedition which conflicts with our plans."

Roofus snorted as he nabbed some more hay. How lucky he was, to not have a care in the world. As long as he had enough to eat, he was perfectly contented. If only I was a horse!

I tightened my fists so hard it hurt. The disappointment cut like a knife inside me. Dad was deserting me for one of his projects yet again.

"Why does this have to happen right now?" I yelled in despair when he told me that he had to leave tomorrow afternoon.

"Because the expedition is starting now," Dad said. "This is my big chance to go on a fantastic journey and make a sensational discovery. I just can't say no. It could be years before I have a chance like this again!"

"But you don't have to go, do you, Mom?" I pleaded. "Couldn't Dad take the pictures himself this once? Then you and I can still go on our vacation as we planned! After all, we've paid for the airline tickets and the hotel and everything..."

But Mom just shook her head. "That wouldn't work," she said. "You know how hopeless Dad is when it comes to photography. It's important that the pictures are good. They're often the deciding factor when it comes to buying the book. And the books are what we live off of – you know that."

I saw the excitement shining in her eyes and knew that it was a lost cause. She was already looking forward to the expedition. My feelings, on the other hand, she evidently did not care much about. A dark, painful wave welled up inside me.

"You don't want to be with me! That's what this is all about. You don't care about me at all! You always go away! Everything else is more important than I am! I hate you!"

"But, Alicia..." My mom tried to put her arms around me, but I pushed her away and ran out of the house.

So here I was, in the stable, not knowing what to do. I did not want to go home, I was sure of that! Most of all, I wanted to stay away until my parents were gone. Good riddance to them!

Maybe I should go for a ride on Roofus? But I didn't really feel like riding right now. I just wanted to hide in a dark

hole and never come out. Maybe I should run away? Then my mom and dad would have to stay home to look for me. But no... I couldn't do that. Grandma would get really scared if I did that. And even if my parents deserved it, Grandma certainly didn't. Besides... what if they didn't miss me at all? What if they just left, without caring whether I was found or not?

Of course they wouldn't do that, but still... I wasn't so sure...
I stayed in the stable for several hours, keeping busy with Roofus. I'm sure he had never been brushed more thoroughly. Shannon, who owns Aramis, the other horse in our little stable, came by briefly to shovel the stall and feed her horse really quickly. She was in a rush, because she was going into town with her mom, to go shopping for summer clothes. I was glad she didn't stay long, because I didn't feel like talking to anybody.

"Have a great vacation!" she shouted as she hurried back out to her mom's waiting car. "And don't worry! I'll take very good care of Roofus while you're gone!"

She left so fast that I didn't have a chance to say anything. Oh well, she'd find out soon enough that our vacation was canceled, and that she wouldn't have to take care of Roofus after all. I shrugged my shoulders. There was no hurry. I could tell her tomorrow... at least that's what I thought when I rode my bike back home a little later. As it turned out, I was totally wrong!

Chapter 2

My legs shook like jelly and I wondered if I was going to faint or throw up, or maybe both. How my mom and dad could look so unaffected after such a horrific plane ride was more than I could understand. They were chatting as cheerfully as if they had just gotten off a ten-minute ride on the bus back home.

But having solid, firm ground under my feet again helped a little. I took a deep breath of fresh, cool air, and felt my dizziness slowly going away. The airport we had landed at was way out in the middle of nowhere, with mountains and tall trees all around. From the air it had looked about the size of a postage stamp, as the small 8-person propeller plane fluttered downward, bouncing like an injured crow in powerful gusts of wind.

"We'll never hit that tiny little air strip," I whimpered while clinging to my dad's arm in panic, clutching so hard that he complained. "We're going to hit the trees and crash! Why did you guys drag me into this nightmare?"

I wished with all my heart that I was back home – in the safe, warm stable with the smell of horse and hay around me.

"I'm going to die now! I'll never see Roofus again!" I thought, shutting my eyes tight to avoid watching as the plane plunged into the treetops.

But the plane didn't crash. It landed without a hitch, and here I was, standing in the most remote wilderness, in a different country, surrounded by an enormous forest. From the air, it had looked like the forest stretched for miles and miles in all directions, with mountains sticking up like an uneven row of teeth here and there. The landscape back home where I had grown up was mostly open plains with only a few scattered clusters of trees. I had the feeling of being closed in among all these tall trees, like I was going to suffocate. When I closed my eyes, I got this weird, creepy feeling that when I opened them again the trees would be surrounding us completely and the airport would be gone. Only tall, looming trees in an endless forest where you could walk for days and days without getting out... I blinked anxiously and looked around, then shook my head. Of course the airport wasn't gone. What a silly idea! I must be in shock still, after all that had happened these last two days.

Was it really only two days since I came home from the stable, sad and depressed because there wouldn't be any island vacation in the Caribbean? It seemed so much longer ago, almost like a different life. I remember kicking my boots off in the entrance, wondering if I should just go straight up to my room and stay there for the rest of the evening. But I was hungry, and besides, I decided that Mom and Dad might as well get to feel the brunt of my anger and disappointment. Serves them right!

The door to the back patio was slightly ajar, and I heard voices out there, even though the curtain was closed. I was about to go out and join them, when the sound of my mom's voice made me stop. "But you've got to understand that we can't take Alicia with us," she said, a trace of budding panic in her voice. "It's impossible!"

I stopped dead in my tracks inside the door. I know you're not supposed to listen in on other people's conversations, but this conversation was about me, so I felt I had a right to know what they were saying.

My heart started beating harder, and I felt a jolt, then a sinking feeling in my stomach, as I realized that Grandma was trying to convince my parents to take me along on the expedition.

"Mommy, sweetheart," said my own mom, "couldn't you stay home with her just this once? Don't you understand how important it is for us to...?"

"Just this once? Is that supposed to be a joke?!" I had never heard Grandma's voice this sharp before. "Don't get me wrong. I love Alicia more than anything in this world. But there is a limit to everything, and I have just reached mine! You know perfectly well that I have already made plans of my own, to go on a vacation with two of my friends. And this time I refuse to change my plans at the last minute, just to accommodate your wishes. Besides, it's about time for you to start taking responsibility for Alicia, and not just leave everything to me! Either she goes with you, or you'll have to drop this expedition. That's all there is to it!"

It got quiet for a while. Then my mom said, obviously directed toward Dad, "Maybe Alicia could stay with Rita while we're gone... I know it's not a great solution, but..."

I didn't wait around to hear any more after that. I ran upstairs to my room, threw myself on the bed, and dissolved in tears. Now I finally knew for sure. I was only a burden to my parents, a millstone around their necks. An unwanted element that they would place anywhere, just to get rid of it. Mom knew very well that I can't stand Aunt Rita, and that the feeling is mutual. Some adults simply don't like kids, and my Aunt Rita is one of them. She has never even tried to pretend...

Just the thought of staying with her for more than two weeks until Grandma came home from her vacation was absolutely unbearable. She's sarcastic, and she makes no secret of the fact that she thinks I'm stupid, immature and boring. Rita is single, and lives in a tiny

one-bedroom apartment in the city. You can barely breathe in there for fear that you might leave a fingerprint in her shiny designer kitchen!

If they come and tell me that I'm going to stay with her, then I'll definitely run away, I thought rebelliously, wiping my tears. I slammed a DVD into the player, and stayed on my bed watching a movie I had seen at least five times already. The familiar story had a lulling effect on me, and I was almost in dreamland when there was a knock on the door, and Mom and Dad came in.

"We've got some great news!" said my dad. "You're coming with us, for your very first wilderness adventure! What do you say to that?" He looked at me with a big smile on his face. If I hadn't known any better, I would have believed that he actually thought it was good news. Mom's smile wasn't quite as convincing, however. I guess she wasn't as good an actor as Dad. Anyway, I wasn't fooled by their smiles. After overhearing their conversation with Grandma, I knew they were forced to take me with them, whether they wanted to or not.

Most of all I felt like screaming at them, and telling them they could go to the end of the universe as far as I cared, and they could go there without me! But the thought of Aunt Rita kept me from saying it. If I refused to go with them, they might just pressure her to take me in. Either that, or Grandma would feel so sorry for me that she would cancel her own vacation after all. I didn't want that. So I just nodded and said okay to everything they said, without really listening.

"It wasn't easy to get another airline ticket, but I finally managed to get one," said Dad, looking as if he expected me to start shouting for joy that he had gone to so much trouble for my sake.

When I didn't answer he cleared his throat, looking somewhat embarrassed, and told me I'd better start packing.

"And take some warm clothes along," said Mom as they left. "The weather can vary a lot in that part of the world."

I nodded and went reluctantly to get my biggest suitcase. Not until I was done packing did I realize that I didn't even know where we were going. This really was an adventure into the unknown, and I was starting to feel a mixture of fear and excitement. Maybe it wouldn't be so bad? Or maybe it would be worse than bad. I envisioned endless days of tiresome walking through a vast wilderness, just waiting for some wild and dangerous animal to jump out from the bushes and have me for lunch. I almost decided to run to Grandma and beg her to stay home with me, but I couldn't do that. I crawled into bed instead, tucking the covers tightly around me while a million butterflies fluttered frantically in my stomach, making it impossible to relax. This was going to be the worst vacation of my life. I could just feel it.

Chapter 3

"Hey, are you okay? You're not feeling sick, are you?" Dad's voice brought me back to the present. He had a worried look on his face.

"No, I was just thinking," I said, squeezing my eyes shut for a moment. "Don't worry, I'm not going to get sick and ruin your important expedition." Even I could hear how sarcastic that sounded.

Dad gazed at me with a frown. For a moment it looked like he was going to say something, but then he seemed to change his mind. He walked over to the airplane, where the pilot was opening a door on the body of the plane. Our luggage was in there.

"Would you help me get our things out?" he shouted over his shoulder.

Reluctantly I went over and pulled out my suitcase and a small backpack, which held my toiletries and horse books. The suitcase was very heavy, and I wondered how I was going to manage everything on the trip.

When I asked Dad about it, he said there would be packhorses to carry our stuff for us. "Do you see that ranch over there?" He waved his arm toward a cluster of trees in the distance. "They rent horses and ponies for hunters and others who need them."

I felt a flicker of joy. Horses! There were horses here. And some of them would

come with us on the trip. Maybe I would have a chance to ride one of them. That would be great!

Dad seemed to have guessed my thoughts, because he said, "The horses will be working on this trip, and they'll be tired from carrying big loads all day, so don't get your hopes up about them. These horses are work animals, not toys."

As if Roofus was some kind of live teddy bear! I gave him an angry glare. Is that what he thinks of me? That I'm a little child who's was just playing with a live toy animal? I could feel myself getting hot inside with humiliation. If he had ever seen Roofus and me at riding events, he might have understood that we actually worked hard. But how would he know? He was almost never home. Had he ever even seen me ride? I doubted it.

Mom came with me to an event once, but as far as I could tell she had shown more interest in the text messages on her cell phone than in watching me ride. She couldn't have made it clearer how little she cared. I didn't ask her to come to any more events after that.

"Where's Adele?" Dad looked around for Mom.

"Over there," I said, pointing. "She's talking to that lady who was waiting by the airstrip when we landed."

Then my mom came walking toward us, accompanied by the lady. "This is Gail," she said, smiling. "She lives on the ranch over there." Mom pointed in the same direction that Dad just had.

"She and her husband, Howard, own the packhorses that we'll be using," said Mom without giving Gail a chance to say anything. "Honey, we may want to ask Howard to come with us on the

expedition. He grew up around here, and Gail says he could show us some fantastic rivers and rapids, as well as some rare birds and a very special breed of beavers, which live in this area."

Dad's face lit up. "Then he might just know something about... the thing that could become the most exciting part of this trip," he said. "I'll go and talk to him right away."

He and Gail left together.

"This is going to be a great adventure!" said Mom excitedly. "But do you know what the best part is?"

I shook my head. Mom was smiling like she was holding a million dollar lottery ticket or something.

"Howard and Gail have a daughter your age. And they have riding horses too, Haflingers, as well as packhorses. Isn't that great?"

"I'm sure it's great for them," I mumbled somewhat confused. "But what's so great about it for us? A lot of people have riding horses."

"They rent out rooms, too," said Mom, "and when Gail told me that, I started thinking..." Suddenly Mom got quiet and didn't look me in the eyes anymore. I got a sinking feeling in my stomach again. Now what was she up to?

I got the answer soon enough. Mom jumped to it. "As you know, this expedition is really meant for adults, and truth be told, you would most likely find it pretty boring. But now I've arranged something much better for you. You'll stay here while we're gone, and you'll be able to ride as much as you want!"

"C'mon, honey, say something! Say you're happy, at least..." Mom sounded unsure. I hadn't said a word to her or Dad for the last hour. Not after I found out that they were going to dump me here at this backwoods ranch in the middle of nowhere. Happy? How could she think that I would be happy? I looked around. It actually looked pretty nice and pleasant here, but I wasn't willing to admit that. That wasn't the point. The point was that Mom, with my dad's reluctant consent, had dumped me here with strangers, people neither of us had ever met before. This is how far she was willing to go to avoid spending time with her own daughter. I was completely crushed and felt so numb inside that when Mom and Dad hugged me goodbye and got ready to leave I didn't react at all.

"We've got communication equipment with us, and we'll contact you regularly,"

said Dad, laying a hand on my shoulder. "Have a good time, sweetheart."

A good time? As if he cared! And he might as well not bother to call. I had no intention of talking to either him or Mom. I turned my back on them and went into the house. A small part of me was hoping that they might come running after me, saying that they'd changed their minds and wanted me to come with them after all. But when I glanced over my shoulder before the front door closed my parents were already out of sight. Clearly they couldn't get out of here fast enough. They'd probably forgotten about me already. I felt a big lump in my throat as I slowly followed Gail up the stairs to the second floor. She opened the door to the first room on the right.

"This will be your room," she said. "My daughter, Suzanne, will come up in a moment and help you unpack." She gave me a warm smile. "Cheer up, sweetheart. Maybe things won't be as bad as you think. I promise we won't eat you, and I think you'll find that we have some really nice horses. Your mom told me what a good rider you are."

As if my mom knew anything about it, I thought bitterly, while trying my best to return Gail's smile. It wasn't her fault that I felt so lonely and abandoned. I felt more alone right then than I had ever been in my life. At the same time I couldn't help feeling a little relieved too, that I wasn't going into that vast, unfamiliar wilderness with a bunch of grown-ups.

Gail left, and I was alone in the room. So much had happened in such a short time that my head felt kind of woozy. I probably ought to be happy that at least I'd come to a place where they speak English, I thought with a flicker of grim humor. At least I knew the language. What if they had taken me to a place where everyone only spoke Swahili, or something like that?

I figured I'd better hurry into the bathroom before Suzanne showed up. Sure enough, just as I finished washing my hands I heard someone on the stairs. I quickly got back to my room just in time to see the door being flung wide open. A whirlwind entered the room and practically attacked me.

"Hi, I'm Suzanne, but you can call me Sue! I could hardly believe it when Mom told me that a girl my age was going to stay with us for a while. And a girl who rides, even! This is great! We're going to have so much fun together! I know all the best riding trails, and we can race, and make hurdles and..."

Apparently she ran out of breath, because she stopped. I was just standing there like a fish with my mouth open, completely overwhelmed by the incredible energy emanating from this gangly body in front of me.

Then I smiled at her, feeling the tenseness suddenly let go of me. I hadn't noticed until now just how uptight and on edge I had been. There are some people, though, who are simply impossible to not like. Suzanne was that kind of a person. Before five minutes had gone by, I felt as if I'd known her for ages. She was funny, easy to talk to, and managed, at least for a while, to make me forget my anger and bitterness. We unpacked my suitcase in no time at all.

"Let's go down and eat," said Suzanne, "then I'll show you the stable and the horse pastures. And we'll have to pick out a horse for you. Do you have your own horse at home?"

I nodded. "His name is Roofus and he's the best," I said, feeling a pang of longing for him. "I've got some pictures of him somewhere among my things. I'll show them to you later."

Suzanne and I went downstairs to have some lunch, and it soon became clear to me that Gail was just as lively and friendly as her daughter. Suzanne's dad wasn't around. Gail told me that he'd already left with the packhorses.

"He's tickled pink about going on this expedition," she said. "Why, with the ranch and all the work around here, he doesn't get many chances to go away on a trip like that anymore."

Gail smiled. "Howard told me that your parents were hoping that he might be able to show them the blue bears."

Suzanne started laughing. "Don't tell me they fell for that tall tale! There are no blue bears. Everyone here knows that!"

Gail noticed the confused expression on my face and explained, "Last fall, two men came here to do some bird watching. We have some pretty rare hawks in this area. Anyway, they claimed to be experienced hikers and all, but nonetheless they ended up getting lost."

Suzanne gave a chuckle. "When they finally showed up one of them told everyone that he had seen this little blue bear up in a hilly slope. It disappeared when he tried to get closer, and they didn't find any trace of it afterwards. A blue bear! Did you ever hear such nonsense?"

"Maybe it had rolled around in some blueberry bushes," I suggested.

"Maybe so. I bet the other bears didn't take long to lick it clean if it came home covered in blueberries!" Suzanne giggled.

Personally, I felt a shudder down my spine. The thought of bears being in the area, blueberries or not, scared me.

After we'd eaten, we went outside to look at the horses.

"This is where the packhorses usually stay," said Suzanne, pointing at the closest paddock. "But since they're gone now, we could set up a hurdle there. Do you know how to jump, by the way?"

I nodded. "Roofus loves to jump, and we actually took first place in a local jumping event this spring. It was great, we had so much fun!"

"That's wonderful!" Suzanne gave a sigh. "I wish I could compete sometimes, but it's way too far to travel with a horse."

"Well, at least now we can compete

with each other," I suggested. But just as soon as I had said it, I felt a nervous tremble in my stomach. I hadn't ridden any horse other than Roofus since I got him. What if I couldn't do it? I suddenly pictured myself riding around the arena, screaming in helpless panic on a horse I didn't know. Why in the world did I have to go and brag about my riding abilities? Suzanne is probably a much better rider than I am. What if I just made a total fool of myself?

"We'll take it easy for a couple of days so that you can get to know the horse," said Suzanne, almost as if she had read my mind.

"Here are the riding horses," said Suzanne as we reached the next paddock. "We rent them out to hunters and other people who are going up the Rangus River to do rafting. Some people like to take both riding horses and packhorses along for the trip. There's a paddock up the river, where the horses stay while the rafters are gone. An old hermit lives up there, and he takes care of the horses and keeps predators away."

My stomach tightened again. "Are there a lot of predators around here?" I tried to make my voice sound relaxed, but I don't think I succeeded.

"There are some bears and wolves around," said Suzanne, "and a few years ago we had a couple of mountain lions wandering about in the forest. They really spooked some rafters who were going up the river. Their guide notified the rangers, though, because the mountain lions aren't supposed to be in this area. It turned out they came from the wildlife refuge some hundred and eighty miles from here. The park rangers came and hunted them down with tranquilizers and took them back to the refuge. Since then we haven't seen any more mountain lions around here, fortunately!"

"But what about the bears, and the wolves..." I said as I glanced at Suzanne.

"It's not very common to see bears in this part of the forest, but last year we had a killer bear roaming around," said Suzanne, and she wasn't smiling anymore. "It tore apart several deer before the hunters managed to track it down. The wolves pretty much stay put over by the mountains. They hardly ever come down here. Only on a few occasions have they come close enough to the ranch that we decided to put the horses inside the stable to keep them safe."

Wolves? Ugh! A whole pack of big, gray animals with sharp teeth and food on their minds! I felt panicked by the mere thought of it. The most dangerous animal I had ever been in close contact with was the neighbor's cocker spaniel. It's an old grumpy dog that snaps at anybody who gets too close. It's tried to bite me several times, but I was never really afraid of it. This, however...

I threw an involuntary glance over my shoulder, as if I expected to see a bloodthirsty pack of wolves right behind me, salivating with hunger and anticipation.

Suzanne smiled. "Did I scare you? I didn't mean to. You're safe here. My mom has some kind of sixth sense when it comes to wild animals. She can feel when one is nearby. And if they come too close to the ranch she or my dad fires a warning shot into the air to scare them away. We've never lost a horse... at least not at the ranch..."

She swallowed, and suddenly got busy telling me all about the different horses. Clearly something had happened that she didn't want to talk about, and that was just fine with me. I wasn't at all sure that I wanted to know. A tragic story wasn't exactly what I needed right now.

"Over there, in the paddock, is Jasper. He's my horse!" said Suzanne proudly. "Did you ever see a more gorgeous horse in the whole world?"

I looked at the horse she was pointing

toward. It was a Haflinger. Not particularly beautiful, but not ugly either. Exactly like Roofus, in other words. I knew perfectly well that Roofus couldn't measure up to the more noble Arabian horses or fullbloods when it came to looks, but to me he was the sweetest, most beautiful horse in the world regardless, and it was no surprise to me that Suzanne felt the same way about Jasper. I felt another pang of longing for Roofus. It wouldn't be the same to ride another horse...

We walked to the paddock. Suzanne whistled and Jasper lifted his head, ears pointed. She whistled again, and he came running toward us, neighing excitedly. Suzanne stuck her hand in her pocket and pulled out three peppermint candies. Jasper stretched his muzzle forward and chomped them eagerly right from her hand.

I let Jasper sniff my hand. He looked a little disappointed not to find any candies there, but when I carefully stroked him across his soft muzzle he snorted happily and flapped his ears.

"Looks like you've been accepted," said Suzanne with a smile. "Jasper's actually a very sociable horse who likes everybody. He's very calm and gentle. The only thing he really hates is loud noises."

I soon got to see proof of that small fact. A girl who looked like she was a few years younger than Suzanne and I came running around the corner of the house, yelling at the top of her lungs, "Yoo-hoo, Sue! Here I am!"

Jasper jerked and laid his ears back flat. His eyes rolled until the white parts showed, and it was clear that he wished he were far away. And who could blame him, I thought. The girl's piercing voice must be downright painful to a horse's sensitive ears.

When the girl saw me, she stopped suddenly. "Who are you?" She stared at me with an expression that was anything but friendly.

"I'm... I..." I stuttered, totally taken aback by the unfriendly look on her face.

"Hi, Lily," said Suzanne, not showing any sign of having noticed the tense moment. "This is Alicia. Her parents are part of the expedition that just left a little while ago. She's going to stay here until they get back. Isn't that the greatest?"

Lily didn't look like she thought it was all that great, to put it mildly. Her mouth closed into a grumpy grin, and she gave me a look that said she wished I'd go to the moon and further. I didn't understand why. I hadn't done anything to her, had I?

"Are you Sue's sister?" I asked, a little confused.

Lily only shook her head and continued to stare at me. So Suzanne answered instead.

"No, Lily is my neighbor," she said. "That is, if you can call her a neighbor when we live two miles from each other." She laughed. "Lily comes here twice a week to ride."

"And Tofu is my horse, so you can't ride him!" interrupted Lily, as if she had just caught me red-handed trying to steal her horse.

"I..." I started, but was interrupted by Suzanne. She looked irritated.

"Of course Alicia won't be riding Tofu," she said. "I've just picked out Silas for her."

"Silas? Are you crazy? He's so difficult to ride!" Lily looked at Suzanne with astonishment.

"Oh, I'm sure Alicia can handle him just fine," said Suzanne calmly. "It's not that he's difficult, he just needs a good, firm rider."

Lily looked unhappy again, as if Suzanne, by saying I was a good rider, had somehow insulted her. I found myself thinking I was glad Lily wasn't going to be around every day. She seemed downright unpleasant to me. But if this was how she was going to be, that was fine with me. See if I cared!

I turned my back on her and focused my attention on Silas instead. He was taller than Roofus, with a wider rump. And he acted a little uneasy and jumpy. Maybe he could tell that I was nervous? At any rate, he took a couple of quick steps

backward when I approached him, as if he was saying, "Hey, stay away from me, I don't know you! What do you want?"

From behind me, I heard Lily's piercing voice, "See? He's backing away already! She'll never be able to control him. You might as well admit I was right."

I felt my anger rising. Who did she think she was, anyway? I'd show her!

Without going any closer to Silas, I started talking to him in a soft, calming voice. I could tell by his ears, which arched toward me, that he was listening to my voice. After a little while I could practically see his whole body become more relaxed. Carefully I took a step closer, still continuing to talk to him. I made sure to keep my gaze partially away from him the whole time, so that he wouldn't feel that I was staring at him in a threatening way. One step closer, then another... Slowly I stretched my arm out toward him. What would Silas do now? My heart was beating hard from the tension. Then I breathed with relief. Silas sniffed my hand, and when I gently let my hand slide across his muzzle and up the ridge of his nose, he allowed me to do it. I took the last step toward him, and Silas stood still and let me pat him on the neck and stroke his flank.

"Good job!" I heard Suzanne say approvingly. "I didn't want to say anything beforehand, because I didn't want to make you nervous or anything, but Silas is always a little skeptical of strangers. Now that he's accepted you, I'm sure you won't have any problem riding him. He's a wonderful riding horse, so you have something to look forward to!"

I smiled and patted Silas on the neck. He snorted quietly and lowered his head to nibble on some grass. That's a sure sign that he didn't feel threatened anymore.

"Did you hear what Sue said?" I mumbled as I continued to pat him and scratch him, though he didn't pay any attention to me anymore. By now he cared more about his food again. "She says that you're a fantastic horse and wonderful to ride. I can't wait. We'll have fun together, you and I."

As I turned around, I caught a glimpse of Lily's face. Her expression was about as sour as if she'd eaten a whole boatload of lemons. What was the matter with that girl? Was she jealous because I had a good handle on horses? Or was it because I was going to live here and be with Suzanne every day?

I shrugged my shoulders. There was nothing I could do about that. I could put up with her for a day, anyway. And tomorrow she wouldn't be here, fortunately. I wasn't going to miss her, that was for sure.

Chapter 4

"You're the world's second sweetest horse, you know that?" I scratched Silas on the forehead and was rewarded with a totally contented look, which showed very plainly how much he liked it. "Only Roofus is sweeter. I hope you don't get offended by my saying that. He's mine, you see, and I miss him..."

Silas didn't look a bit offended. He waved away a fly with his tail, nodding his head lazily, as if he was about to fall asleep.

The day before, after her mom had picked up Lily, I had tried to ride him. And I was glad Lily wasn't around, because she'd certainly have found plenty of fuel for sarcasm. It had taken a little time to convince Silas that it was okay for me to ride him. At first he made all kinds of leaps and bucks, trying to get me off. If Lily had been standing there watching I probably would have fallen off from sheer nervousness. But, encouraged by Suzanne's approving comments, I had managed to hang onto his back. Finally, Silas calmed down and accepted me as his rider.

"I hope we don't run into any wild animals," I told Suzanne as we saddled up the horses. We were going for a ride, and I had mixed feelings, both looking forward to it and dreading it.

"It depends on what you mean by wild animals," said Suzanne, smiling teasingly. "We may very well run into a few deer, even if Dad says there are unusually fewer of them in the woods right now. He thinks they've moved further south, maybe because the wolves have been more bothersome than usual."

She shrugged her shoulders. "The good thing about that is that the biggest packs of wolves usually go after them, which means that we can feel safer around here. Besides, wolves hardly ever attack humans. Or horses either, really, at least not when there are people around to look after them. It's a different story if they're alone..." She stopped and it looked as if she shuddered.

My heart was beating hard against my chest. I could tell that Suzanne was thinking about whatever it was that had happened, and she didn't want to talk about it. I wondered what it was. Had one of the horses run away from the ranch? Had the wolves attacked it?

This time it was my turn to shudder. I thought about Mom and Dad who must be well into the backcountry by now. Did they sleep under open sky? What if wolves, or scarier yet, a bloodthirsty killer bear, was sneaking around their camp at night? Were my parents in danger out there?

"If so, they brought it upon themselves," I mumbled to myself while tightening the girth and giving Silas one last

cuddle before I swung into the saddle. "Nobody forced them to go way into the wilds on some ridiculous search for blue bears!"

But I couldn't quite manage to get rid of the worried feeling in my stomach while Suzanne and I rode down the trail leading past the airport. Eventually it occurred to me, however, that it wasn't my parents I was worried about at all. They were in a group of eight people traveling together, and probably had plenty of weapons on hand. It was myself I was worried about. How could I be sure that Suzanne was right? What if the wolves were still here, starving because

all the deer had left the area? It sent chills up my spine just thinking about it, but I didn't dare say anything to Suzanne. She would probably just think I was even more of a wimp than she'd already realized. I'd better keep my fears to myself and try to make the best of this. I wasn't used to life in the wilderness, that's all. Maybe things would get better after a few days.

There was nobody at the airport, and the tiny airstrip looked eerily deserted, as if no airplane had ever landed there. I was already dreading having to get on that puny little plane again to go back home. But there was no point in thinking about that now. At the moment I wanted to enjoy this ride, or at least try to enjoy it.

That was easier said than done, however. I was nervous, and jumped at the faintest sound around me. The whole time I expected something scary and dangerous to appear between the trees – like a big, ferocious hungry animal, eying a delicious horse steak for lunch. Of course Silas could sense my nervousness and was affected by it too. He started thrashing uneasily with his head, stepping sideways while neighing and snorting in an agitated way. This was no good; I'd better pull myself together.

"Take it easy, boy," I said, trying to make my voice sound calm and firm. "There's nothing to worry about. Everything is fine..."

No sooner had I said it than a shadow came shooting out from the trees in a jumble of fluttering wings and brown feathers. Before I knew what had happened I was lying on the ground looking befuddled as a big bird – was it a hawk? – managed with great effort to take off with its prey. A large, rat-like animal dangled from its powerful beak.

I sat up slowly, rubbing my shoulder, which hurt, but otherwise I seemed to be in one piece. I was just a little shaken and shocked, and it felt as if my heart was in my throat. Silas! Where was Silas?

I almost started crying with relief when I saw that he hadn't run off. He was standing beside Jasper, breathing heavily, his legs scraping the ground, looking as if he might want to run off at any moment. But Suzanne had a firm grip on his reins and was talking soothingly to him. I stumbled toward them because my legs were trembling so hard.

"I'm... I'm so sorry," I stuttered miserably.

"It wasn't your fault!" Suzanne looked at me with big eyes. "That hawk came flying out of nowhere, flapping its wings right in front of Silas's nose! I'm surprised he didn't panic more than he did. If that had happened to Jasper, he would have gotten so scared he'd have thrown me off in an instant and run straight back to the ranch. It's actually happened before, that he's been scared senseless like that. I had to walk a long way to get back home."

Suzanne grinned and patted Jasper. I took Silas's reins from her and started stroking him slowly and gently on the ridge of his nose. His ears were still laid flat back against his neck, so I knew I'd better be careful and not do anything that could spook him again.

"You don't need to feel bad," said Suzanne. "Accidents happen. And everything is okay, right? You weren't hurt, were you?"

I shook my head. "No, except my shoulder hurts a little. Nothing to worry about."

I almost started telling her that Silas had been jumpy and uneasy before the hawk scared him, but I didn't. I just promised myself that from now on I would be calm and steady and keep my fears under control. Silas wasn't going to be nervous because of me, at least.

I knew it wasn't going to be easy to keep such a promise, because the forest, with all its secrets, still scared me. But I was determined to manage it. We waited until Silas was completely calm again before we continued riding. Suzanne told me that some of the largest trees farther inside the woods were more than a hundred years old.

"One of these days we'll ride to the old forest," she said. "It's a very special feeling to stand underneath an old tree like that and look up. You feel like the tree reaches all the way to the sky!"

I nodded without saying anything. I wasn't so sure that I really wanted to ride further into the woods. But I didn't tell her that. I didn't want to prove to her what a scaredy cat I actually was. Later I came to regret this bitterly, not having said what I was thinking, because it was the trip to the old forest that started it all... the awful, terrifying series of events that lay ahead. But of course I didn't know that then.

Chapter 5

"See there?" Suzanne pointed. "Those are the oldest and tallest trees in the entire forest." We held the horses back. It had been a long ride on a winding path through rough terrain. I had no idea how Suzanne managed to find her way, but she said she had been here many times, so I guess one eventually learns the way. And it had been a nice ride regardless, because I'd been at the ranch for five days already, and wasn't so scared anymore. Suzanne and I had already taken several long rides along different paths, and since no scary animals had shown up on any of those occasions, my fear had kind of melted away by itself. I started looking forward to our rides. Silas really was a wonderful horse, and I had gotten increasingly fond of this beautiful, robust gelding who carried me so sturdily and surefooted through the most uneven terrain. The only drawback was Lily. Whenever she came along on a ride I had to bite my tongue to keep myself from screaming at her to be quiet. Her shrill voice was always cutting through the woods and was just about as irritating as the continuous wailing of a male cat in heat late at night.

She could talk nonstop about absolutely nothing. How Suzanne stood having her around all the time was more than I could fathom. Maybe I wouldn't have minded her quite so much if she had been nice to me, but she wasn't. She had at least stopped throwing sarcastic remarks at me, after Suzanne got mad and thoroughly told her off one day, but she still gave me the cold shoulder and acted hostile. I tried my best to ignore her, but shutting her out completely wasn't easy.

"Would you like to go over to the tallest tree and stand underneath it? I'll hold Silas for you."

Suzanne looked at me. I shrugged my shoulders. I didn't really understand what the big deal was with these trees. All right, so they were old, but I could see that from here. And I could see that they were tall as well. But hey, if it was so important to stand underneath one of them, I was willing to give it a try. I was about to hand the reins to Suzanne when Lily said, "Why don't we tether the horses and go over to the trees, all three of us? I haven't stood underneath one for a long time. And I'd like to make a wish."

"Make a wish? Do you mean to say that they're wishing trees?" I looked at her with surprise.

At first Lily looked like she didn't want to tell me, but then she nodded. "It's just an old legend, of course," she said. "My great-grandmother told me that if you stand underneath the tallest trees in the forest, look up toward the sky and wish for something, your wish will come true. And the best thing is if you have three people under three trees."

"The part about three people is news to me," said Suzanne with a laugh. "But why not? It only takes a second, so it couldn't hurt to leave the horses here for a while. Then we can sit down afterwards and eat our lunch."

We tethered the horses and took their saddles off so they could get some fresh air on their backs. It had been a fairly warm ride in the nice weather. Then we all walked over to the tall, old trees. They sure had a lot of moss growing on them. Funny to think that they've been here for more than a hundred years, I thought, laying a hand on the rough tree trunk.

"Hold on a sec, I just want to double check that I tied up Tofu properly," said Lily. "Since we can't see the horses from here, I don't feel so sure now."

She ran off. While we were waiting for her to come back I noticed that one of the mountain peaks that we could see from here was different from the others. It looked like a giant had taken a big bite out of it. When I commented on it to Suzanne she said, "It must be a result of the earthquake last summer. My dad told me that there were several big rockslides up in the mountains. The earthquake was so powerful that some of the windows in our house broke, and the old barn on the neighboring ranch collapsed."

"Do you have a lot of earthquakes here?" I said in a weak voice. Yet another thing to worry about on top of the wild animals.

Suzanne shook her head. "No, that was the first one in fifty years, so you don't have to worry about that."

I looked down, feeling embarrassed. Why was I so afraid of everything? Why couldn't I be cool and brave, like Suzanne? She must think I'm completely hopeless, even though she's too nice to say it out loud. For once I was relieved when Lily showed up.

"All in order!" Lily was short of breath. "Now I'm ready to make a wish."

I leaned toward the knobbly tree trunk and looked up. From this angle the tree seemed to be endless, as if it reached all the way to the sky, just as Suzanne had said. I held my breath and felt almost dizzy. Should I make a wish? It was probably just some old superstitious nonsense, but it couldn't hurt either.

I closed my eyes. "I wish... I wish that my parents would show some interest in me... and show that they love me!"

I silently repeated my wish three times. Because if it helped to be three people under the trees, then maybe it helped to repeat the wish that many times too.

When I opened my eyes again, I felt

kind of stupid. Imagine standing here under a tree, thinking that my parents would ever change. There was a sting in my chest. Over the last few days I'd actually had so much fun that it had kept the sore thoughts away. Suddenly the disappointment and anger welled up inside me again, like a dark wave of sorrow. I swallowed as I felt the tears coming. Not for the life of me was I going to let Lily see me cry. I quickly pushed myself away from the tree trunk.

"I'll go over to the horses real quick," I said over my shoulder, and almost ran back to where we had tethered them. I felt an enormous urge to bury my face in Silas's safe, warm coat. He could comfort me, just

like Roofus usually did. I could almost feel the good, warm smell of horse already.

I glimpsed the horses between the close-growing trees.

"Hi, Silas! Here I am," I said softly, as I rounded the last tree blocking my view. "Did you miss... " The words got stuck in my throat. Two horses' heads turned and looked at me. Two heads, not three! Silas wasn't there anymore!

"I just don't understand this," I said, probably for the tenth time. "I tethered him properly. I know I did! So how can he be gone? And where is he?"

I scouted into the forest, desperately hoping that Silas would suddenly appear from behind a tree. But the forest was

ominously quiet around us. No sound of neighing or horse's hooves...

"If you had tethered him properly, he wouldn't be gone now, would he?" Lily's voice had an accusing tone. I shrank inside. Was she right? But I was so sure...

I closed my eyes, trying to recall the moment. Silas had stood by the tree, nibbling on a tuft of grass. I had thrown the rope around a thick branch and made a knot... and then another one... or hadn't I? Had I been so preoccupied by the thought of going to the wishing trees that I had forgotten to make a safe knot? The more I strained my brain to remember, the more uncertain I became...

"You should have done what I did!" Lily's irritating voice made me open my eyes again. "I went back and double checked Tofu's tether, just to make sure

that he was safe. Now you can see how smart that was!"

I glared at her with hostility. Silas was gone! Did she have to gloat about it? You'd almost think she was happy about me having screwed up. Wasn't she the slightest bit worried about the poor horse that was now out there all alone and unprotected? What if there were dangerous animals nearby? Suzanne had said there weren't, but still... how could she be so sure of that?

"You don't have to rub it in, Lily," said Suzanne. She looked irritated. "Can't you tell how sorry Alicia is? I didn't double check Jasper's tether either, so on that account Alicia and I are even-steven. And as I remember, you were the one who forgot to close the gate to the paddock only a couple of months ago, letting

Jasper and Tofu into my mom's vegetable garden. You don't have to act so superior. Everyone can make a mistake."

Suzanne turned to me and pretended not to see the insulted look on Lily's face.

"Don't worry about it," she said. "I'm sure Silas went straight home when he noticed that he was free. He probably got tired of waiting."

I felt a pang of relief at Suzanne's words, and at the way she was taking it. If somebody had let Roofus loose in the thick of the woods, I'm not so sure that I would have been as calm about it. But Suzanne seemed to be used to their horses finding their way home on their own. I remember she told me that Jasper had

done that after he had thrown her off. But wasn't it a little strange that Silas had just left the other two horses and gone back alone? Suddenly I got all worried again.

"C'mon," said Suzanne, "stop looking so worried, Alicia. I guarantee you that when we get home Silas will already be there."

I hoped she was right. We hurried up and got Jasper and Tofu saddled. Silas's saddle had to be left behind. Suzanne and I covered it up with branches and sticks, hoping it would be safe until we could pick it up. Then we rode home. Lily looked angry as I got on Jasper's back behind Suzanne. I couldn't help wondering why Lily disliked me so much. Not that I liked her any better, but at least I tried to act polite toward her. Lily didn't even bother to try. And now she seemed to be disappointed that Suzanne wasn't angry with me. I simply didn't understand her. But it was all right with me if she wanted to be a sourpuss all the time! That was her problem, really. Besides, I had more important things to worry about right now.

During our ride home I kept scouting the surroundings, hoping to see Silas standing somewhere along the trail waiting for us. But there was no sign of him, nor of any other animals either, which at least I was happy about. But how could Silas find his way home alone in this thick, confusing forest? I had no idea how Suzanne did it, but she seemed convinced that he would find the way, and she ought to know what she was talking about.

I really tried to relax, but the closer we got to the ranch, the more worried I got. What if Silas wasn't there? What if he was lost in the woods and we never found him again?

Gail was just rounding the corner of the house when we turned into the farmyard.

"Hi!" she said cheerfully. "You're home already? I hadn't expected you guys back for a while yet."

Then her smile disappeared. "Did something happen?" she asked. "Why are you riding double on Jasper? Where's Silas?"

"We thought he'd be here!" Suzanne's voice tensed up. "He got loose from the tether... we thought he'd run back home. Isn't he here?"

Gail shook her head. "I haven't seen him since you guys left."

My stomach tightened into a knot, and when I slid down from Jasper's back my legs felt all numb and funny. Silas hadn't come home! He was gone! All the fearful thoughts that had gone through my head on the way home suddenly became brutal reality. Silas was missing. He was somewhere in that huge forest, all alone and defenseless. How would we find him?

A horrible vision of Silas desperately fleeing from a pack of hungry wolves went through my mind. "It's my fault! My fault!" I wasn't aware of saying anything until I heard my own voice. "What if Silas never comes back... what if the wolves get him?" I sniffed, as tears started trickling down my cheeks.

Everything seemed hopeless. My parents were deep in the wilderness, I was here among people I didn't really know, and now I had managed to lose one of their horses. They would hate me if Silas didn't come home again. Maybe they hated me already! What if Gail got so mad that she threw me out? Where would I go then?

But Gail didn't say an angry word to me. Instead she came over and put her arms around me. "Don't worry, it'll be okay," she said softly. "Horses have a very keen sense of direction. He may still come home..."

I leaned toward her and gave in to an uncontrolled, violent crying jag, which felt like it would tear me apart. Gail mumbled comforting words, but I didn't hear them. I was so desperately unhappy and felt such guilt, and I had no idea how to handle it. Life would never be all right again, I was sure of it! Silas, had to come home! He had to!

But Silas didn't come home.

Chapter 6

A silent, velvety dark of night descended outside my window. The bed was soft and comfortable, but I couldn't relax. I couldn't stop thinking about Silas. Where was he? Was he safe? Or had wild animals already snuck up on him and... and...

I shuddered at the horrible pictures forming in my mind. Gray, furry beasts with shining eyes and salivating mouths, approaching without a sound, mercilessly circling their prey, an unsuspecting, unprotected horse.

"No!" I sat up in bed. It was too horrible to think about. The wolves couldn't take Silas! I would never get over it if he were killed. It would be my fault! How could I have been so careless?

We had been riding around in the woods looking for Silas all afternoon. I had borrowed a horse whose name I couldn't even remember. Gail had come too, as had Lily's dad. His name was Frank, and he was an excellent tracker, Gail told me. We split up into two groups. Gail rode with Suzanne and me, while Lily went with her dad. I was glad I didn't have to see her for a while, even though she hadn't said a word since we got back to the ranch. It looked like she had finally recognized the gravity of the situation, because she had dropped the sarcasm and nagging about not having double-checked the tether.

At some point I thought I saw Silas, and my heart jumped for joy, but it turned out to be just a deer that got scared and ran off into the woods when we got closer. I was so disappointed, I felt like screaming out loud.

Eventually it started getting dark, and we had to go back home. I had a little hope that Silas would be at the ranch when we got back, but he wasn't. We just had to accept that he was still gone.

As I lay down in bed again I closed my eyes. I really needed to get some sleep. I wanted to be alert the next day, because we would be going out to look for Silas again.

"Hundred and ninety-nine sheep, hundred and ninety-eight, hundred and ninety-seven..." I tried counting sheep backwards in an attempt to relax. When I got down to forty-five sheep, I finally started dozing off. My body was slowly relaxing... – forty-four... forty-three...

"AWOOOOOOOO! AWOOOO!"

At first I didn't realize where the strange sound came from or what it was. But then I came to with a start. My eyes popped open, and my heart

leaped all the way to my throat. Wolves howling! There were wolves out there, and they didn't sound very far away either. I got goose bumps all over.

"AWOOOO!" There was another howl from a different part of the woods.

Why did they howl like that? Could it be because... because... I shuddered. Did wolves howl when they had caught a prey? I didn't know. All I knew about wolves was that they were large, gray and dangerous... at least when there were many of them. And this sounded like a whole bunch! A whole pack of them!

If they were hunting right now, what kind of animal had they trapped? Was it a deer... or... or...?

"Oh, please, please, pretty please!

Don't let it be Silas," I mumbled to myself. "Please let him be safe tonight, far away from the wolves, so we can find him tomorrow and get him home!"

I imagined Silas walking through the woods, with his reins dragging behind him on the ground. What if it got caught on a bush? Then he couldn't even run away if a wild animal picked up his scent. He would just be standing there... totally helpless... while the predators came closer and closer...

Even if it was all in my imagination, I thought I could feel his fear.

My hands tightened into fists as I desperately wished that my parents were back from their expedition. But wishes don't help any. I knew that from before. So why had I wasted time standing under that idiotic tree wishing for something that would never come true? If I hadn't done that, Silas would have been safe now.

If Mom and Dad hadn't dumped me here, maybe I would have had a horrible time going on that expedition with them – but that would have been a lot better than sitting here in an unfamiliar house in the middle of the night, all alone and scared. And I didn't dare to go knocking on Suzanne's door either. It was so quiet in the house that she was probably asleep. And even though she had said she didn't blame me for what happened, I wasn't totally convinced of that. I might be the last person she wanted in her room right now.

Why weren't my parents ever there when I needed them? Dad had said they would call, but he had probably forgotten. How typical! He was probably too busy looking for those blue bears. Blue bears! What a super idiotic idea! What would be next? Pink penguins?

I don't know how long I sat there, tense, listening to the mournful, terrifying howls. But eventually they stopped, and I must have fallen asleep, because the next time I opened my eyes it was light outside, and I was lying in an unnatural, twisted position across the bed. I whimpered as I tumbled to the floor. One of my legs was completely numb, and there was an unpleasant prickling in my toes. I limped into the bathroom to take a shower and get dressed, eager to get out and start looking for Silas. We just had to find him today! And for some reason I suddenly felt sure that we would. Silas would be back, alive and well, and then I could get rid of this awful feeling of guilt.

But even though we looked all day, we didn't find Silas. Gail had called a local search and rescue agency, and a helicopter had flown over and searched the area for a couple of hours. They frightened the horses every time they came sweeping through right above us. I rode the same horse as the day before, and still had no idea what its name was. I just couldn't think of anything but Silas.

"I was so sure that we were going to find him today," I said, on the verge of tears, when we finally were forced to head back. Most of all I would have liked to continue looking, even though I was so tired that my eyes burned and my body ached. My rear end was sore and every muscle in my thighs and legs were aching. I wasn't used to sitting in the saddle for so many hours at a time, so it was pretty hard. But if I could bring Silas back safe and sound, it would be worth a lot more pain than this, I thought.

As it was, the only thing we brought back with us was Silas's saddle. Lily's dad picked it up and brought it back. He and Lily had gone to the oldest part of the forest looking for tracks that might tell them in what direction Silas had gone.

"We tried to follow some horseshoe prints that we found," he said when we met back at the ranch. All of us were pretty worn out and downhearted. "It looked like they led toward the mountains, but then they disappeared and we couldn't find them again."

"I'll ask the helicopter to sweep through there tomorrow," said Gail, stroking her hand through her hair. "We'll try everything, even if..." She stopped, casting a quick glance toward me.

I felt like a clamp tightened around my heart. I knew very well what she was going to say. With every passing day, the chances of finding Silas alive were getting smaller. The thought of him alone in the forest another night, surrounded by howling and hungry wolves, was unbearable. If he was still alive, that is! But he had to be! Silas couldn't end up as food for the wolves. He couldn't!

I felt like running upstairs to my room and burying myself under the covers. But that wasn't an option. The horses needed to be cared for after our long and strenuous ride.

"If you guys could take care of the horses, Frank and I will go inside and fix dinner," said Gail. "I think we all need some good nourishment after such a long, hard day."

We did as she asked and started brushing the horses. It was hard to even lift my arms, but I didn't dare complain. I had been worried that Lily would bombard me with sarcastic remarks again as soon as her dad and Gail left, but she didn't say a word. She brushed Tofu in a fast and automatic manner, before starting to brush her dad's horse. I noticed that she frequently stroked the back of her hand across her eyes. Was she crying? That's actually what it looked like. Apparently she was just as sad as Suzanne and I were about Silas being gone. Nothing strange about that, of course. After all, she had been coming here a couple of times a week for a long time. So naturally she knew all the horses and was fond of them.

"Do you think we'll find Silas?" I asked Suzanne.

She turned toward me, holding the grooming brush in her hand. "I don't know," she said with a grave look on her

face. I regretted having asked. This wasn't the answer I had been looking for. I wanted reassurance that everything would be okay.

"If he's still in the forest, he's probably okay," continued Suzanne. "But if he's gone toward the mountains, like Frank thought..." She stopped and swallowed. "That's where the wolves hang out, you know... so I just hope that Frank is wrong. The thing is, he's usually right..."

She swallowed again, and I saw that there were tears in her eyes now. "That's where it happened last time..."

I felt a chill go through my whole body. "What last time? What happened?" I had a strong feeling that I was going to regret having asked, but I couldn't help myself.

"It was two years ago," said Suzanne. "My dad was out with a group of hunters. He was showing them which area they were allowed to use for the deer hunt. Something happened which scared the horses. One of the hunters was thrown off, and his horse ran off in a panic. It ran toward the mountains. This was late in the afternoon, and it had started getting dark, so they had to wait until the next day to start looking for it. Dad and the hunters spent the night in the forest. He said he feared the worst when he heard the wolves howling in the mountains..."

"Did they find the horse?" I asked, in spite of not really wanting to hear anymore.

"They found it... well, they found what was left of it..."

"Do you mean... the..."

Suzanne nodded. "The wolves had caught it and eaten most of it..." She shuddered. "I'm just glad I wasn't there to see it. Fortunately, that's the first and only time we've lost a horse that way. At least until now..."

"Don't say that!" Lily's voice sounded shrilly over the paddock, making me jump. I had almost forgotten she was there. When I turned around I saw her standing there with a wild look on her face, staring at Suzanne.

"Don't say that Silas is dead, killed by the wolves! He's alive! I know he's alive! He can't be dead! He can't be...!"

"I'm sorry, Lily, I was just..."

Suzanne didn't get a chance to say any more. Lily suddenly turned around and ran away, into the barn.

Suzanne and I looked at each other.

"Gosh, she's sure taking this hard," Suzanne said finally. "And I didn't even think she cared that much about Silas..."

"I understand how she feels," I said. "Just the thought of Silas being dead gives me the creeps, not to mention a big lump in my throat. I don't want it to be true either! If he dies, it's my fault!"

Suzanne shook her head. "You can't think like that," she said, sounding just as grown-up and sensible as my grandmother.

"I can't help it," I sniffled, head down, feeling the urge to do as Lily, and run into the barn where I could hide in a corner. "What happened is just unbearable! I don't understand how you can be so calm when poor Silas might be eaten by a pack of bloodthirsty wolves!"

"If you had grown up in the wilderness, as I have, you might understand it better." Suzanne stroked Jasper across the muzzle and looked at him. He stood there calmly eating grass, blissfully ignorant that one of his friends may have become wolf food.

"Of course I'll be terribly sad if something has happened to Silas," she said. "He's a great horse, and if... if the worst has happened, I'll miss him and grieve over him. But when you live as close to nature as we do, you know that it can sometimes be brutal. That's just the way it is. The wolves are carnivores. They don't kill for fun or to be mean, but for food, in order to survive. They're part

of nature, and they have a right to live too! The wolves have no way of knowing that a horse is any different from a deer. To them it's just a good meal..."

She looked straight at me, and suddenly I felt like a stupid, sniveling, little child. I quickly dried my tears. Enough of this sobbing. If Suzanne, who had known Silas for years, could be calm about this, then I should be able to as well.

But it wasn't easy. I could feel the tight knot in my stomach through the whole meal. There was nothing I could do about it. And apparently I wasn't the only one who felt this way. Lily refused to come in and eat with us.

"I'm not hungry," she shouted when Suzanne tried to get her to come inside with us.

After we had eaten, Frank went out to get her and take her home. He and Gail had agreed to wait until after the helicopter had gone over the area between the old forest and the mountains before continuing our own search on horseback.

I had thought we would be riding out at the crack of dawn, and I wasn't sure if I was disappointed or relieved. It would be nerve-wracking to just sit around doing nothing to try to find Silas. At the same time I was so utterly exhausted that the mere thought of another long day sitting in the saddle seemed impossible. I hoped the people in the helicopter would find Silas. Then I was willing to ride however far it might be, regardless of how tired I was. With all my heart, I wished to find him, alive and well! It was too soon to give up hope. But what would happen if they didn't see any sign of him? I didn't dare ask Gail about that. I was too afraid of what the answer might be.

Chapter 7

It was a tired threesome who crawled into bed that night. I took a long shower first because I was sticky with sweat and felt totally beat. Even so, I had no hope of falling asleep yet. I was lying there waiting to hear those terrifying, horrible howls at any moment. I didn't care what Suzanne said; I felt that I hated those wolves. How could they not understand the difference between a horse and some other animal? I knew I was being ridiculous for thinking like this, but I couldn't help it.

"Please, oh, please," I whispered to myself. I wasn't sure who I was talking to, exactly. Maybe the moon. It was hanging outside like a shining plate in the sky. "Let Silas be safe. Make the wolves find something else to eat... Please!"

It was a full moon that night. Isn't that when wolves are especially dangerous? No, how silly; the full moon had something to do with werewolves, not real wolves. And werewolves only exist in fantasies and fairytales, fortunately. It was certainly bad enough with real wolves... hunting together...

Just now they were circling around the tree down on the ground. I clung to the branch, terrified that I was going to fall. When did I climb up into the tree? I couldn't remember. And where had these furry, frightening beasts come from? They hadn't been here a moment ago... The pack circled quietly around Silas, their amber eyes shining with a hungry expression. The terrified horse ran back and forth in a panic, trying to get away from the enemy, but the wolves surrounded him on all sides.

They were closing in on him, getting closer and closer...

I woke with a start. My heart was beating like a hammer against my chest, and my back was soaked with sweat. Thank heavens it was only a dream, a horrible nightmare. Or wasn't it? The dream could easily be true, as far as I knew. I shuddered as I got out of bed, stiff in every joint. Ouch! I was sore in muscles I didn't even know I had!

I looked at the time. It was almost ten o'clock! I had slept like a rock the whole night through. The morning was well underway, and the helicopter was probably out searching already. They might even have found Silas! I hurried into the bathroom. I was itching with anticipation and impatience... and more so, of anxiety. What if they didn't find him? Or worse yet, what if they found...

No, I refused to think like that. Today was another day and another chance to find Silas. When I came downstairs to eat breakfast, however, I found out that it was the last chance. Suzanne had already eaten, but she sat down to keep me company.

"The helicopter left an hour ago," she told me. "So now we just have to cross our fingers and hope they see him."

"What happens if we don't find him today, either?" I swallowed the last bite as I looked at Suzanne. There was something in the expression on her face that gave me the answer before she said it.

"Then it's over. There won't be any more searching. We can't keep looking forever without knowing where to look..." She shrugged her shoulders and didn't say any more.

I didn't say anything, either. I just hoped even more than before that they would find him this time. After all, Frank had seen tracks that led toward the mountains, right? Any moment now, we would get the good news. I just had to believe that.

Lily showed up while we fed the horses and cleaned up in the paddocks. She didn't look like she had slept much. She also seemed nervous and upset, and started working with rapid, jerky movements, constantly glancing up at the sky as if she thought the helicopter would suddenly be right above our heads without us having heard it. I knew very well how she felt; at least I thought I did. But when I tried to say that to her, she hissed at me, "Stay away from me! I don't want to talk to you! You don't understand anything!"

Her violent reaction took me by surprise, and I did as she said and kept my distance. It felt like a very long wait. When the helicopter finally came back, flying low right above the treetops, I felt as if we had been waiting for days.

Gail heard it too and joined us outside. "Let's just hope they have good news for us now," she said, smiling. Her smile looked a little tense, I thought, as if she didn't really believe that they would have found Silas.

The helicopter landed on the airstrip and went out of sight. I wanted to run over there, but Gail stopped me. "Don't bother, they'll come to us," she said. "I promised to have some food ready for them when they were done searching."

I was impatient and thought they took way too long, even though it probably wasn't more than ten minutes from the helicopter landing until two men showed up.

"Hi, Gail!" shouted one of them cheerfully. "I really hope you have a strong cup of coffee for a tired helicopter

pilot and his confused sideman. Stephen, here, might just need a whole pot to himself, by the way. He's so tired he's seeing things!"

Stephen, the younger of the two, looked embarrassed. "And I'm sure Robert isn't going to let me hear the end of it as long as I live," he said, nodding toward the helicopter pilot. "Why didn't I just keep my mouth shut? Next time I'm not going to tell him a single thing about what I see!"

Gail looked confused. "What exactly did you see?" she asked Stephen.

Stephen looked down and didn't seem too eager to answer, but Robert started laughing hysterically. Between gasps of laughter, he managed to say, "He saw... he claims that he saw... a blue bear! How crazy is that?"

Stephen blushed and looked even more uncomfortable.

Suzanne and I looked at each other. I felt funny inside. A blue bear? Was it possible? I thought it was just a silly story that somebody had made up... But now...

"I know, it was probably just the morning light playing tricks on me," said Stephen when Robert had finally stopped laughing. "But when I saw it there, out on the side of the mountain, I could have sworn it was blue. I'm not joking. Unfortunately it got scared by the sound of the helicopter and disappeared before Robert could see it."

"Was it a big bear – like a grizzly?" asked Gail.

Stephen shook his head. "No, it looked like a regular black bear," he said, "except that it was much smaller, about the size of a sheep, and it –"

"... was bluuue!" Robert started chuckling again. This was apparently the funniest thing he had heard in a long time. "A cute little blue, miniature bear!

Now do you see why this boy needs some strong coffee? He must be hallucinating from the exhaustion!"

I was itching to ask if they'd seen Silas, but at the same time I was scared of the answer. If they had seen him, wouldn't they have told us right away, and not started joking around about tiny little blue bears?

"Did you see any sign of the horse?" It was Gail who asked, as if she had read my mind.

Robert got serious again. "We saw something," he said. "But I couldn't tell for sure if it was a horse or a big deer. It was..."

"You can't tell the difference between a horse and a deer? Are you stupid or something?" It was Lily who interrupted. Her voice was even sharper than usual, and Gail looked at her with a mystified expression. Before she could say anything, Lily continued.

"Please, say it was a horse you saw, please say it was Silas! He has to come back! He has to!"

Lily crouched down, totally desperate now, and I saw that she had tears in her eyes. My own heart was beating hard. What if it was Silas they had seen? I hoped so; I hoped it with all my heart. But the next moment I hoped just as badly that it wasn't Silas they had seen, because Robert said, "The animal we saw was lying on the ground, partially hidden under some branches. It was impossible to get a good look at it, but it was definitely dead! And considering that the missing horse has been out there for two days and two nights now..."

"Nooo!!!" Lily screamed so loudly that I jumped. "No! Silas can't be dead! How can you even suggest such a horrible thing? I hate you!"

"Lily! What's the matter with you?" said Gail in a shocked voice. "You shouldn't talk like that. And it may not..."

But Lily didn't listen. She sprinted toward the barn.

Gail wanted to go after her, but Robert

stopped her. "Leave the girl alone," he said calmly. "This has obviously come as a shock to her. Give her some time to collect herself. We can't be certain that it was the horse we saw, so there's no need to draw any conclusions yet. She'll see that too, when she gets a chance to think it through."

Gail nodded. "You're right," she said. "Let's go inside and get you some food, then I'll go and have a talk with her before Frank and I ride out and check the spot where you saw the dead animal. Are you coming, girls?"

Suzanne and I followed slowly behind them. We heard the distant sound of the

elephone ringing inside the house. Gail
an on ahead to answer it. When we got
nside, she was standing by the phone,
houting so loudly it reverberated
etween the walls. She nodded toward me
s she held the phone out away from her
ar. "It's your mom," she said, "on a very
ad connection. That's why I'm shouting.
he and your dad are having a grand
ime, apparently. She wanted to know
ow we're doing. Here, do you want to
alk to her?"

I took a step closer to the phone.
uddenly I had a strong longing to hear
ny mom's voice. But then I stopped. All
he bitterness and frustration I had felt
velled up inside me again. So she and
Dad were having a grand time, huh?
Naturally! They weren't dragging along
heir bothersome daughter! And then they
hought that as long as they just gave me
 call, I would rush to the phone and be

overjoyed to hear from them. No way! I'd
show them!

"Thanks, but no thanks," I said,
turning away from the phone. "I don't
want to talk to her, and you don't have to
tell them hi from me either."

"But, don't you want... "

I didn't wait to hear any more, but
went straight into the dining room and
sat down at the table. For a moment I
was tempted to run back to Gail and tell
her I had changed my mind, but instead I
clenched my teeth together in stubborn
determination. If Mom and Dad didn't
want me along, I didn't want to talk to
them, and that was that! Let them have
the stupid expedition to themselves, and
run around in all the wrong places
looking for their blue bears. See if I
cared!

Maybe I should have talked to Mom
anyway, to tell her that Stephen said he

had actually seen a blue bear? It didn't seem very likely that he would have made it up, when it was obvious that neither he nor Robert had ever heard any rumors about the blue bears before. What if there really were such things as blue bears? If my parents had heard what Stephen said, they would have gone totally bananas with sheer excitement.

I felt a pang of guilt, but brushed it aside. It wasn't my fault that my parents had rushed off to the wrong place. It served them right! I could always tell them the next time they called... if they bothered to call any more, that is...

Gail came in, telling me that my mom and dad both said hi. I mumbled a thank you without really meaning it. She gave me a questioning look, but didn't say anything. I was glad about that. I didn't want to talk about my parents.

I wasn't hungry at all, but to be polite I helped myself to a little bit of stew. It was probably good, but it might as well have been cardboard. That's how little attention I paid to what I was eating. I was trying to forget about my parents and push them into some place in the back of my head. I couldn't handle any more right now when I was so worried about Silas. Was it he that Robert and Stephen had seen? Was he dead? I felt sickened by the mere thought of it, and put my spoon down, unable to take another bite. I imagined Silas, the gentle and beautiful horse, lying still on the ground, dead because I had been careless enough to not tie him up properly. How could I have been so thoughtless? It was completely unlike me. I closed my eyes, picturing how I had tethered Silas to the branch before taking

his saddle off. What had I done next? Suddenly another picture appeared in my memory. I saw myself double check the knot before I followed Suzanne and Lily over to the old forest.

My heart jumped at the memory. Had I really checked it, or was it just wishful

thinking because I couldn't stand the thought of it being my fault that Silas was gone? What if it was a real memory, that I had double-checked the knot? No, I couldn't have, because then Silas wouldn't have gotten loose... unless...

A vague, unpleasant thought started forming in my head. I thought about the way Lily had been acting since Silas had disappeared. Why would she be so overly distraught? Silas wasn't her horse. Of course she could easily love him dearly anyway, but still... there was something odd about it...

The sound of a door shutting made me open my eyes with a start. I had been so absorbed by my own thoughts that I adn't noticed that the others were done ating.

"Were you sleeping?" Suzanne smiled t the bewildered look on my face. You've been sitting here with your eyes losed, looking like you were far off in Dreamland."

"No, I... I was just thinking," I said. There's something I want to talk to you bout, but not here..." I glanced at Robert nd Stephen, who were drinking coffee nd talking excitedly about some fishing rip they were apparently planning. Gail asn't there.

"Well, we could go out to the horses," uggested Suzanne. "Mom went to the arn to see if Lily wants some food now."

"It's Lily I want to talk to you about," I aid as we approached the paddock where asper was standing, seemingly dozing. I elt a huge lump in my throat. Silas should ave been there too, but instead he was lost n the woods somewhere, maybe even...

"Where's Tofu?" Suzanne interrupted ny sad thoughts. "He's not here. You lon't think Lily could have gone off iding by herself, do you?"

"Maybe she rode back home," I uggested, just as Gail came out of the barn.

"I can't find Lily," she said with a vorried look. "I'm a little worried that..."

"Tofu is gone," said Suzanne. "She nust have taken him for a ride."

Gail frowned. "Alone? She knows erfectly well she's not allowed to ride off he ranch by herself. I don't understand vhat's going on with that girl. But she'll et a piece of my mind when she gets ack! The last thing we need right now is or something to happen to her or Tofu. I ope she has enough sense to stay on the rail around the airport, at least."

Gail shook her head with an angry expression. "I'd better go and call Frank right away. Regardless, we need to ride out to take a look at..." She stopped, and I knew she had been about to say "Silas."

I was glad she didn't. If she didn't say his name, I could still pretend that it wasn't Silas lying out there in the woods. Besides, it was far more likely that it was a deer, wasn't it? There're tons of deer out there, and only one horse... It would probably be a lot easier for the wolves to attack a deer...

"What did you want to say about Lily?" asked Suzanne after Gail was out of earshot.

"I think that... I'm not sure, but... and maybe you'll think this is just something I'm saying to cover up my own careless-ness... but, I think that maybe she did it..."

I stopped, not really knowing how to continue.

Suzanne had a confused expression on her face as she looked at me. "Will you stop talking in riddles? I don't understand what you're saying. What did she do?"

"Loosened the tether! I know it sounds totally crazy, but I'm getting more and more certain that I really did check that it was properly tied. So how did Silas get loose? I can't prove anything, but..."

"... You're saying that Lily set Silas loose." Suzanne finished my sentence for me. I couldn't interpret the expression on her face. Did she believe me, or...?

"She certainly had the opportunity to do it," I said quickly. "When she went back to check on Tofu. It wouldn't have taken long to loosen the knot..."

"But why would she do a thing like that?" Suzanne looked at me.

"Because I think she's very jealous,

and doesn't like the fact that I've gotten to ride with you so much. Maybe she was hoping that your mom would get so mad that I wouldn't be allowed to ride anymore."

Suzanne thought about it for a while, then she said, "I don't really want to think something like that about Lily, but I have a feeling you may be right. That would also explain her strange behavior these last couple of days. She's been completely out of it since Silas disappeared. Lily knows that the horses normally run right home if they take off, so if she did set him loose she would have counted on him taking the quickest route back to the ranch."

"Where do you think she is now? Do you think she...?"

Suzanne nodded. "I'm willing to bet that she didn't just go for a regular ride. I think she's gone to the place where Robert said they saw the dead animal."

"But isn't that dangerous?"

Suzanne nodded. "It's not very smart to ride into the woods alone, and

especially not without a signal gun to scare off predators with, in case there are any..."

Suzanne didn't say any more, but my own imagination had no problem conjuring up visions of Lily, alone and defenseless among wild animals sneaking up on her and Tofu...

"We'd better tell my mom right away!" Suzanne ran toward the house. I stayed where I was. My legs were shaking and I felt a mixture of fear and anger. I was angry, no, I was furious with Lily for what she had done. At the same time I was scared to death that something awful might happen to her out there in the woods. Then I remembered the helicopter and felt a pang of relief. How lucky that it was still here! Robert and Stephen would find her in no time at all. At least I hoped so. And when she got back, I was going to let her have it, I thought murderously. What she had done was simply too despicable! I wasn't going to let her off easy for this!

Chapter 8

"I just don't know where she could be!" Suzanne stroked her hand over her eyes.

What we had first thought would be a quick and easy search had turned into anything but.

"If Lily doesn't want to be found, it would be easy enough for her to hide every time she hears the helicopter," Gail commented after Suzanne complained about the search taking too long. "Maybe we have a better chance of finding her.

I suggest that we first ride to the place where they saw the dead... uh... deer," she said with a quick glance at me. "I'm guessing Lily is somewhere in that vicinity. At least I'm hoping she is."

So did I, and the faster we found her the better. Every last muscle in my body was protesting when I got back in the saddle of the horse I had been riding the day before.

"Uh, what's this horse's name, by the way?" I asked Suzanne quietly, feeling a little bad about not having bothered to find out before.

His name, it turned out, was Rigoletto. A rather odd name for a horse, if you ask me! I bent forward and patted him on the neck. Rigoletto was a very stable, calm horse that didn't get scared by the static from walkie-talkies or the shouting of the other people who were helping us search for Lily. I was glad about that. The thought of a trip through the air and a hard landing was even less appealing than usual, because of my excessively sore joints and muscles.

It felt like we'd been riding for an eternity when we finally arrived at the spot where Robert said the dead animal was. We hadn't seen any signs of Lily and Tofu.

"It must be somewhere right around here," said Gail, scanning the area. "Probably behind the brush over there."

She pointed and I felt my heartbeat quicken. What if Silas really was lying there? I held Rigoletto back while Gail rode down the difficult path. I was not going with her. I didn't dare, because I didn't think I could handle it. Suzanne started riding after Gail, but seemed to change her mind.

"If that turns out to be Silas, I'd rather not see him," she said. "It's bad enough if it is a deer. Have you ever seen a deer that's been killed by a predator?"

I shook my head. "No, and I have no wish to see it, either. I can only imagine how disgusting it must be. What about you?"

Suzanne nodded. "I've seen it a couple of times... it's not a pretty sight... and it always makes me think about our horse, the one I told you about who was killed... ugh... I don't want to talk about it anymore."

I didn't blame her, especially now that the same thing might have happened to Silas. Poor old Silas! And everything was Lily's fault, I felt increasingly sure of that. When I get my hands on that girl...! But we had to find her first.

Could she possibly have been here already? Had she seen Silas lying there, dead and cold under the trees? If so, what was she feeling now? How would I have reacted if I had found him?

I scratched Rigoletto's mane, thinking that I would have been beside myself with grief and guilt. I would probably have wished that nobody ever find me! Was that how Lily was feeling right now?

And all of a sudden the hatred, which had been steaming inside me throughout the ride, was gone. Poor Lily! She must be going through an absolute nightmare right now, all alone and miserable. Of course she hadn't ever meant for things to go so wrong, even I understood that much. She had never planned for Silas to die.

I had tears in my eyes. The picture of Silas, lying still under the trees, was suddenly more real than the warm, live

horse I sat on. The tears trickled down on my hands and I started shaking all over. Would Gail leave Silas lying in the woods and let the wolves finish him off? Was he almost eaten up already? That was a horrible thought, and I felt another wave of nausea.

I pondered these questions so hard that when Gail called I didn't hear what she said at first. But then her words sank in, and I started crying harder, this time with relief. It wasn't Silas, it was a deer! All hope was not gone! We might still find him alive!

Right then, all thoughts of Lily were forgotten.

"I just can't imagine where she would be!" said Suzanne, possibly for the twentieth time. "Isn't it strange that we haven't seen a single trace of her?"

She peered into the sky, where the sound of the helicopter was a constant, distant buzz. The guys were making their last sweep before they had to return to base. It would be getting dark soon, and we would have to ride back without finding Lily.

Gail kept in contact via walkie-talkie with the other parties that had joined the search. They didn't have much to report. It was starting to look as if Lily had disappeared without a trace, as if a UFO had come and kidnapped her and taken her away to a different planet.

"Maybe she didn't ride this way at all," suggested Suzanne finally. "What if she went back to the ranch, and is wondering where we've all gone? Meanwhile, we're riding around here aimlessly!"

Gail shook her head. "We left a walkie-talkie and a note for her, telling her to contact us if she shows up. And we haven't heard from her. No, I think she's here somewhere. I just wish I knew where, so we could find her before it gets dark!"

Suzanne and I looked at each other. The thought of Lily and Tofu staying out in the woods all alone the whole night was a frightening thought. Nothing in the whole world could get me to spend the night out here, that's for sure. At least that's what I thought then. If I had known what lay ahead, I would probably have climbed into the nearest treetop and demanded that the helicopter pick me up and take me home immediately. Instead I rode on behind Gail and Suzanne, feeling pretty disheartened, on a path that would lead us to the foot of the mountain, and then back to the ranch. I didn't think for a second that we would find Lily there, or Silas either. There wasn't a horse's footprint in sight anywhere.

Visions of my nice, soft bed back at the ranch became more alluring the further we rode. I was more tired than I had ever been in my life, and even though we had taken a break to rest and eat just a couple of hours ago, I was so hungry my stomach was making noises.

I heard static from Gail's walkie-talkie. She answered, and though I couldn't catch more than her part of the conversation it was enough to make my heart start beating faster. "Is it really true?" she said. "Back at the ranch? Almost as good as new? Oh, that's great! What a relief! Thank you for letting me know. We really needed some good news right now!"

"Is it Lily? Is she back at the ranch?" asked Suzanne excitedly when Gail turned toward us.

Gail shook her head. "Not Lily," she said. "It's Silas. Frank and his party stopped by the ranch just now. I think Frank was hoping that Lily would be there even though she hadn't made contact. Silas was standing in the farmyard munching on grass as if nothing had happened. He's in the paddock now and, best of all, besides a few scrapes and minor cuts on his legs, he looks just fine!"

Chapter 9

wish we could tell Lily that Silas is all right! But how can we, when we can't find
r?"

Suzanne held Jasper back as she looked at Gail. "Do we really have to go home?
n't we stay and keep looking for just one more hour?"

Gail shook her head. "You guys are so tired you're swaying in the saddle," she said.
Besides, it'll start getting dark in an hour or so. I want you two to ride straight home, and
l follow in a little while. There's just one more place I want to check before I head back."

"But... " started Suzanne.

"No buts about it," said Gail firmly. "Do as I say, now. You know the way. I hate the
ought of Lily spending the night out here, but we can't really achieve anything more
day. Let's just hope that she'll come to her senses and ride home when she realizes it's
tting dark."

"But what if something's happened to her?"
jected Suzanne. "What if she's hurt?"

"There's no reason to think the
orst at this point," said Gail. "It's
uch more likely that she's
ding. She may even be near
e ranch. We don't know
at she rode into the woods
all. We can't be sure of
ything, however, so
ep an eye out for tracks
hen you ride home."

Then, without waiting
r any answer, Gail
rned her horse and
de away.

Suzanne and I had
ery intention of doing as
e said, but only half a
ile down the path heading
me, Suzanne suddenly
claimed, "Hey! Look over
ere! Do you see that?"

"What? Where?" I stared
ncomprehendingly at her.

"Over there. Look at those broken branches, and look at the ground!"

I looked, and my heart jumped. It definitely looked like something big had ploughed through there, in between the dense growth of trees, and on the ground we could see the faint prints of horseshoes. Was it Silas who had been here, or...?

"Mom! Come back! We found some tracks!" Suzanne yelled so loudly that Jasper jumped, startled. Rigoletto barely moved his ears. I couldn't help smiling. How much would it take for him to react? I wondered. If anybody had hollered like that near Roofus, he would have leaped into the air. Maybe Rigoletto was hard of hearing.

Nobody answered. Gail was evidently out of earshot already. Suzanne shrugged her shoulders. "Okay, then we'll have to check it out ourselves."

"But, we were supposed to go straight home," I reminded her. "What if it's just Silas's old tracks? And it'll be getting dark soon..."

"Yes, but what if it was Lily and Tofu?" interrupted Suzanne. "We can't just go home and not do anything about it."

"No, I guess not," I said reluctantly. I knew Suzanne was right, but the possibility of not making it home before dark terrified me. What if the wolves showed up... or a big bear? What if...

"Relax," said Suzanne, as if she had read my mind. "We have time for a short sweep through here before riding home. It looks like the tracks are heading toward the mountain. Wouldn't it be great if we actually found Lily?"

"Maybe we should try calling out to her to tell her that Silas is all right?" I suggested.

"Good idea," replied Suzanne. "Why don't you do the shouting? Rigoletto doesn't get scared as easily as Jasper. Ride on ahead of me and shout away."

I did as she said. Every hundred yards or so I yelled as loudly as I could, "Liiily! Can you hear me? Silas came back – he's okay!"

But if Lily heard us she didn't answer, and when we got closer to the foot of the mountain slope we lost the tracks. We rode back and forth looking for them, but didn't find them again.

"This is no use. We'd better give up," said Suzanne at last. "Besides, you'd think Lily would have answered if she was in the area. Let's go on home and hope she shows up soon."

"Maybe she's home already," I said,

relieved that we were finally leaving the woods.

I had just tightened the reins to turn Rigoletto around when it happened. A deep, growling sound came from a nearby thicket, making Rigoletto point his ears and stop dead on the spot.

"What was that?" I said, feeling my heart jump all the way to my throat. It sounded like a cat, a big cat. But what kind of cat could be out here in the woods, except...

The chilling truth was revealed when I caught a quick glimpse of yellow and brown fur. A mountain lion! And it was only a few feet away from us! It must have sneaked into the thicket without us noticing it. And now it was getting ready to attack! At least I assumed it was, and apparently so did Rigoletto. Before I could think another frightened thought, he laid his ears back flat against his neck and gave off an ear-splitting neigh that echoed through the forest. Instinctively I grabbed hold of his mane for support, and not a second too soon. He turned like a flash and ran like the wind. I could do nothing but hang on for dear life. My ears were buzzing. I've never been so scared in my life. The airplane ride, which I thought had scared me half to death, was like a Sunday stroll in comparison.

I laid myself flat against Rigoletto's neck, praying for dear life that he wouldn't stumble, that I wouldn't fall off... or get hit by branches. I didn't dare turn around to see if Suzanne was coming. What if...

But then I heard her voice. "Hold on!" she bellowed. "Give him free rein!"

I wasn't aware that I had been pulling on the reins. I managed to loosen them a little. Trees and bushes flew by in a whirl and I felt dizzy. I realized that I was

holding my breath. I took a few gasping breaths and closed my eyes. There was nothing I could do, anyway. I just had to trust Rigoletto to get me away from that terrifying, yellow predator.

At the sound of the hoofbeats changing, I opened my eyes. We were at the edge of the woods, heading up the side of a mountain. Around me was open country. Would the mountain lion follow us here? I wondered. I risked a quick glance over my shoulder. Suzanne and Jasper were right behind me. Jasper was foaming at the mouth, thrashing his head back and forth as if he thought that would

get rid of the pursuer.

But there was no pursuer anymore, at least none that I could see. The mountain lion was gone. Had it followed us at all? I had no idea. Had there actually been a mountain lion, or was it just my wild imagination playing tricks on me? Yes, of course there must have been. Why else would Rigoletto have reacted the way he had? He, who was always so calm.

It looked like Rigoletto sensed that the danger was over, because he slowed down without me having to ask him. When he came to a full stop his flanks were heaving from the wild ride through the forest, and I slid down from his back, my legs shaking violently. For a moment I thought they wouldn't carry me, but they did. I leaned into Rigoletto, whispering into his mane, "And I was wondering what it would take to scare you. Now I know!"

I started laughing, a gasping, unnatural laughter. And in the next moment I started bawling, tears streaming from my eyes. They trickled into Rigoletto's coat, which was already wet from sweat, and I was reminded of

the day I was standing in Roofus's stable doing the exact same thing. Was it only a week ago? It seemed like an eternity... so much had happened since then. I felt a desperate longing for Roofus and the safety of my own home. How my mom and dad could think that wilderness adventures were fun and exciting was totally beyond me. If I ever got back home I was never going to leave again, that was for certain.

I wiped the tears from my eyes and turned to Suzanne. She must have thought I was a complete idiot, the way I was sobbing and carrying on. She, who was used to this kind of life, must have barely been scared at all.

But I was wrong. Suzanne was sitting on the ground, holding onto Jasper's reins with one hand. The other hand was shielding her eyes, and I could tell she was shaking like a leaf.

"Sue?" I said quietly. "Are you okay?"

Suzanne nodded without looking up. "Just give me a couple of minutes," she said, "then maybe my legs will carry me again. I've never been so scared in my entire life. I was sure that mountain lion was going to jump right at us. It was close enough to do it. If it hadn't been for the horses..."

She fell silent. I swallowed, feeling the horror grab hold of me again. We had been in mortal danger, prey to a hungry mountain lion! I almost pinched myself, because it all felt totally unreal. Things like this don't happen, except in movies... do they? But this wasn't a movie. This was real. It occurred to me that it could have been this mountain lion

that had attacked and killed the deer. Or maybe the woods were teeming with mountain lions. What if a whole pride of them had escaped from the wildlife refuge this time? How were we going to get home now? No way was I about to ride back down into the forest again. I glanced up at the sky where a lonesome hawk was gliding, scouting for suitable prey. A chill crept up my spine. It seemed like every animal in the woods was on the prowl. Then I noticed that the sky had started getting a slight glimmer of gray. I realized that we no longer had any chance of making it home before dark. The darkness came so fast around here, much faster than back home. What were we going to do? Did we have to stay here tonight? Oh, no! The thought was unbearable. But what choice did we have?

"Why didn't I take the walkie-talkie my mom wanted to give me?" Suzanne's voice interrupted my thoughts. "Then we could have called for help. Now we have to stay here. We can't ride back through the forest as long as we don't know if the mountain lion is still prowling around down there. And what if there's more than one?"

"That thought had already occurred to me," I said with a shudder. "We'll have to stay here, won't we?"

Suzanne nodded.

"But isn't it dangerous? I mean, didn't you say that the wolves live near the mountains?"

Suzanne nodded again. "We'll have to gather up some firewood and make a campfire," she said, getting to her feet. "All wild animals are scared of fire. A fire will keep them away."

"Are you sure?" I wasn't easily convinced.

"Absolutely sure!" Suzanne tried to sound firm and confident. I hoped she was right. But as she said, what choice did we have?

"C'mon then," I said quickly. "Let's get started, and gather up the biggest pile of dry branches this mountain has ever seen! No wild animal is going to get anywhere near us or the horses!"

Chapter 10

Did you hear that?" I nudged Suzanne, who mumbled
and turned over. How could she manage to sleep
out here, with the darkness all around us so
full of scary noises? I certainly couldn't.

I glanced over at the horses as they
stood nearby, dozing. In the light from
the campfire they looked like
mysterious creatures from another
world. Only the low snorting was
familiar and comforting,
convincing me that it really was
Jasper and Rigoletto standing
here.

We had made camp in a
small thicket growing in a
track along the lightly sloping
mountainside. After we had
made sure that neither wolves
nor mountain lions were lurking
in between the trees, we set up
camp. There was a grassy spot
where the horses could eat, and
fresh water bubbled straight up from a
crack in the rocks. We ran eagerly
toward the water and drank greedily before
we let the horses have a turn. Suzanne assured
me that it would be safe to drink the water, and it
tasted delicious!

Afterwards we gathered up a big pile of sticks and dry branches
for a fire, and ate the leftovers of our bag lunches. As darkness
enveloped us I desperately wished I were somewhere else, in a
safe place with a soft bed and no wild animals.

"Do you think they're out there looking for us now?"
I asked hopefully, while we were making sure that
Jasper and Rigoletto were properly tethered.
There weren't going to be any more horses
on the loose in the wilderness.

59

Suzanne shook her head. "I wish I could say yes, but I highly doubt it. There isn't much point in going out to search when it's pitch black."

"But they can see our fire!" I objected, fully aware of how timid and wimpy my voice sounded. I couldn't stand the thought of being stranded out here all night.

"They have no way of knowing that we're up here on the mountain, even though we've made a fire," said Suzanne, as sensible as always. "They probably think we got lost in the woods. I'm sure my mom counts on us having enough sense to stay put until morning. They'll definitely come as soon as day breaks. If they knew that there are mountain lions on the loose, though, they might actually have tried to find us tonight. But they don't."

I felt like screaming in protest, but I knew that Suzanne was right, so I kept quiet. When it came right down to it, I should have been happy that at least I wasn't alone, like...

"Lily!" I exclaimed, feeling a pang of guilt for having forgotten all about her in the midst of what had happened. "Do you think she's still out here somewhere?"

Suzanne shrugged her shoulders. "I wouldn't be surprised if she's back home slurping hot cocoa right now. Wouldn't that be the ultimate irony?"

"I'm glad you can joke about it," I said pretty sullenly, but then I had to laugh. It really would be quite ironic if Lily were on her way, safe and sound, to a nice warm bed, while we, her rescuers, had to spend the night on a cold, hard rock!

Right then it didn't actually feel so bad, sitting by the warm campfire. We had eaten, not all that much maybe, but at least we weren't hungry, and there was plenty of water and grass for the horses, and enough dry wood for the fire. So maybe the night wouldn't be so bad after all.

But that's what I thought before Suzanne went to sleep. After she dozed off I started hearing all kinds of strange noises. I tried to tell myself that it was all in my imagination, or at least all sounds from harmless creatures, but I still jumped every time I heard something. When Jasper – or was it Rigoletto? – suddenly gave a loud snort I almost screamed before I realized what it was.

The time went by extremely slowly. It was still several hours before dawn, when we could expect to be rescued. I threw more wood on the fire and pulled my jacket closer around me. Maybe I should try to get some sleep too, to make the night go by faster? I lay down and closed my eyes. They were burning with tiredness. The ground was hard and uncomfortable, and I wished more than ever that I were lying safe and sound on a soft mattress underneath a warm, cozy comforter. But it felt wonderful to close my eyes and let sleep gradually take over.

What was that sound? I sat up and listened. Everything was quiet. Had I dozed off and only dreamed that I heard something? I wasn't sure. Suzanne was lying next to me, sleeping as unperturbed as before. Lucky Sue!

My heart beat hard and fast, while I strained my ears. I thought there had been something familiar about the sound, or was that just my imagination too? I had just started relaxing when suddenly I heard the sound again, a kind of hard, clopping sound. It was repeated a few times, then it disappeared and was gone again, but then it came back, closer, much closer this time.

I bent over and tried to shake Suzanne awake. "Wake up," I said. "Somebody's coming... or something... I don't know, but I think..."

"Hmm?" Suzanne sat up, peering drowsily at me. "Why did you have to go and wake me up? I was sound asleep!"

I grabbed her arm and signaled for her to be quiet. "Listen!" I whispered.

Suzanne looked at me. "It sounds like... a..."

We both stared into the darkness, where two silhouettes, appearing against the night sky, came closer to the fire, accompanied by a very familiar clippety-clop sound. Next to the biggest silhouette was a smaller, thinner figure...

"Hello," said a hesitant voice.

"Lily!" Suzanne jumped up and ran toward her. "We've been so worried about you! Are you okay? Where have you been?"

When Lily came into the light from the fire, leading Tofu, I gave a start. She looked terrible. Her hair was all tangled and her face was grimy with dust and dirt. Her jacket was way too thin for a cold night in the mountains, and she was shivering with cold.

"Come here and sit by the fire and get warmed up," I said, reaching my hand out to her.

"But Tofu... "

"I'll take care of him," said Suzanne. "There's grass and water over here."

Lily dropped down next to me and stretched her hands out toward the fire. "Ah, that feels wonderful," she said, but she was still shaking like a leaf.

I took off my jacket and tucked it around her.

"Thank you," she said, turning away. "I don't know why you're so nice to me.

Don't you know what I've done to you? And to Silas!"

She hid her face in her hands as she let out a gasp. "I looked all over," she said, "but I couldn't find him. I was hoping... when I saw that the dead animal was a deer, and not Silas... But he's gone... we'll never find him again... never! And it's my fault! I was the one who untied him and chased him away. I was hoping that Sue would be so angry that she would never ride with you again. I didn't think Silas would get lost! I thought he would run straight home! And now he might be dead, all because of me being so stupid and jealous!"

If I was still harboring any thoughts of revenge, they died then and there. Poor Lily! She had certainly been punished enough for what she had done. I put my

hand on her arm. "Don't worry, everything will be okay. Silas is safe. He came back to the ranch earlier today, and he was hardly injured at all."

"I don't believe you. You're just saying that to make me feel better," said Lily with a sniffle.

"It's the truth," said Suzanne. She had tethered Tofu next to Jasper and Rigoletto, and was coming back to the fire. "Silas is fine. You're the one we've been worried about. We've been looking for you all day, both on horseback and by helicopter. Where in the world have you been?"

"I heard the helicopter," said Lily, looking at us. The tears made stripes down her cheeks. "But I didn't see it. It never came over to the valley were I was hiding. I was glad about that then, but later, after I got hungry and cold, and..."

"Haven't you eaten anything since you left?" I glanced guiltily at the saddlebags. Suzanne and I had eaten all the leftover food. There was nothing left for Lily. Unless...

"Wait a minute," I said, picking up one of the saddlebags. "If I remember correctly, Gail might have stuffed a box of chocolate cookies in here before we left. I forgot all about them."

It was lucky for Lily that neither Suzanne nor I had remembered the box of cookies, because if we had there wouldn't have been a crumb left, I thought as I fished it out. Lily wolfed down the cookies ravenously. When the box was empty we showed her where she could drink some water. The cold water made her chilly again, so we threw more wood on the fire. The flames went high. It was a beautiful and comforting sight, I thought, especially when we heard the first howls of wolves. Fortunately it sounded like they were far away, but what if they came closer? Then the fire would be the only protection we had. Would it be enough to keep them away?

I trembled and moved closer to Suzanne, feeling grateful that I wasn't alone out here in the wilds. I couldn't bear to think how Lily must have felt when the darkness descended on her and Tofu was her only company. Not that he wasn't good company, but a horse couldn't protect her from dangerous predators that may be lurking about. It could have gone really badly.

"Lucky for you that we ended up here on the mountain and lit a fire," said Suzanne just then, as if she had read my thoughts. "Did you see our fire from your hideout?"

Lily nodded. "Or rather, I saw it as I came out from my hideout. At first I thought I was seeing things, but then I realized it must be people nearby, maybe a hunter or somebody like that. I had no idea it was you guys. What are you doing here, anyway?"

"That's a long story," said Suzanne. "We'll tell you all about it, but first I want to know where you've been. How did you manage to hide from the helicopter?"

"I was hiding in the bear valley," said Lily with a shrug of her shoulders. "Well, actually I first thought it was a cave..."

"What?" Suzanne and I stared at her, equally at a loss for what she was talking about.

Lily smiled for the first time since she found us. "I came across a crack in the mountain, which looked like it might be the entrance to a cave," she explained. "And I don't know why, but I thought maybe Silas could be in there. Anyway, I decided to check it out. There was just enough room for a horse to get through the entrance. I led Tofu through, but the entrance didn't lead to a cave at all. It was more like a tunnel, and when I came

out on the other side I saw a valley below. You know what? The blue bears really do exist! They live in that hidden valley! I thought it was just a bunch of nonsense when Stephen insisted he had seen a blue bear. But now I've seen them for myself! They look exactly like black bears, except that they're much smaller, and with a definite blue tint to their fur."

My mouth fell open as I stared at her, then I started laughing. "Oh, that's just priceless," I gasped. "My parents have gone off way into the wilderness with a large expedition to look for the blue bears, and then we stumble across them right here! I think I'm going to die laughing!"

Suzanne watched me with a strange look on her face. She obviously didn't see why it was so hilarious that my parents had gone on a fruitless expedition. But I

was still hurting over the way they had treated me, and couldn't help gloating a little at the fact that they weren't going to find what they were looking for.

"Well, you haven't exactly stumbled across them," she said dryly. "We haven't even seen them. Only Lily has."

"Yes, but we'll do something about that," I said, wiping away tears of laughter. "Let's go and take a look at them as soon as it gets light... while we're waiting for the cavalry to come and rescue us."

"Can't we just ride home on our own?" said Lily confused. "Why do we have to wait for someone to come and rescue us?"

"For the same reason we ended up here on the mountainside," said Suzanne. "You see, we found out that there are more than wolves around here..."

Chapter 11

"Pinch me, or I'll think I'm dreaming!" I turned to Suzanne, but she neither heard nor saw me. Her gaze was fixed upon something at the bottom of the valley, and she looked almost hypnotized by what she saw.

"How beautiful they are!" she said dreamily. "And Lily was right, they really are blue! I wonder why. I mean, bears are usually black or brown! Well, except polar bears, of course. And why are they so small?"

"Perhaps they evolved over hundreds of years," I suggested, wishing I had paid more attention in science class when we were learning about genes and that kind of stuff. "The valley seems to be totally isolated from the rest of the area, surrounded by these tall mountains. I think the crack we came through might be new. Maybe it appeared after that earthquake you told me about. That would explain why hardly anybody has seen the bears. The valley may have been completely sealed off until last summer."

"Mm-hm," said Suzanne distractedly, and I wasn't sure she had heard a word of what I said.

"The bears have probably had all they needed of food, water and shelter in here," I said thoughtfully, "so there's no reason for them to go anywhere else, even if a few of them apparently have wandered

outside now and then, after the crack appeared."

I looked down at the bears. From up here they looked like cute, little teddy bears. I felt like climbing down the steep slope and going over to pet them. But of course I couldn't risk that. They were probably bigger up close, and they may not appreciate the company at all. Or maybe they would be delighted to see a

two-legged breakfast walking right up to them. If they were meat eaters at all, that is. Maybe they just ate nuts and roots and berries? I wondered. Not all bears eat meat, do they? Maybe they do. I wasn't sure.

I could have stood there all day watching the peculiar bear tribe, but eventually we had to go.

"That's the most magnificent thing I've ever seen!" exclaimed Suzanne as we returned to the camp where Lily was waiting. She had stayed behind to look

after the horses. "Imagine, we have such rare and special animals right here, only a few miles from our ranch, and we didn't know about them."

"Just wait until people find out," said Lily. "There'll be a constant stream of curious people coming to see them. It will be the end of all peace and quiet in that secret valley, that's for sure! Which is a pity, when you think about it..."

"Yeah, I didn't think about that," said Suzanne. "But we have to tell somebody about them, don't we? And besides, people will soon discover them regardless. They've already been seen, even if nobody quite believes it yet."

"I think..." I started, but didn't get a chance to finish, because just then we heard the sound of a helicopter approaching, and a few seconds later it appeared above the treetops. We started waving our arms and jumping up and down. The helicopter did a sweep right above us, and we saw a hand waving. Then it flew away again.

Suddenly I noticed how hungry I was. Hungry and tired. It sure would be wonderful to get home, to some good food and a soft, nice bed, safely away from growling predators.

As we led the horses down the mountainside, we heard voices in the forest, and shortly after we saw two people on horseback coming toward us. It was Gail and a man I hadn't seen before.

"Daddy!" shouted Suzanne. "What are you doing here?"

She rushed down to her parents while Lily and I followed at a little slower pace.

"We've been so worried about you!" Gail pulled her daughter into a tight hug. "I tell you, this has been the worst night of my life! I didn't know if you guys were okay, or... But apparently you are,

and you've found Lily! How did you manage that? Are you all okay? Girls, you must be as hungry as wolves," she ranted, not giving us much of a chance to answer any of her questions.

"Don't mention wolves," I mumbled with a shudder. "We heard enough of them last night. Luckily they kept their distance, but still..."

Gail opened her saddlebag and pulled out a sack that contained a few sandwiches with bacon and lettuce. They looked delicious and tasted even better. Grandma always says, "Hunger is the best cook." Now I know what she means. It was the best breakfast I've ever had.

"We made a huge fire," said Suzanne after we had wolfed down the food, "so we were actually pretty safe. But yesterday, when the mountain lion appeared, that's a different story..."

Gail, who was just closing up her saddlebag, stopped in mid-motion. "Mountain lion? Are you saying...?"

Suzanne nodded, and we both started speaking at once about what had happened and how we had ended up on the mountainside.

"I'm sure glad I didn't know anything about this last night," said Gail, shocked. "I would have been even more worried than I already was. A mountain lion! I thought the wildlife refuge had secured the park against any more escapes, but apparently not!"

"We'd better notify the park rangers and try to find out if this one's alone or if there are several," said Suzanne's father, Howard. "But that can wait. Right now, the important thing is to get you girls home."

While we were riding toward home,

Suzanne asked again, "Dad, why are you back home already? I thought you were supposed to stay with the expedition for several more days. Did something happen?"

"Yes, we had a little accident," said Howard, turning in the saddle. He looked straight at me, and I felt my heart skip a beat.

"Did something happen to my parents?" I asked with concern. "Something serious?"

"No, no," Howard said, smiling. "It's just that the trip was cut short after your mom fell out of a tree. She wanted to take pictures of a beaver dam from above, but got too far out on a branch, and it broke. The others stayed behind to study the beavers a little closer, but your mom didn't feel so good after her fall, so I took her and your dad back to the ranch."

"Is Mom hurt bad?" I was on the verge of tears, thinking about how I had said I hated her. That wasn't true at all. I didn't hate her, of course I didn't. I loved her, even though I hadn't told her so in a very long time. What if she had died in that fall? Then I would never have had another chance to tell her.

"No, she'll be fine. The doctor's been here and checked her out," said Gail quickly. "She's pretty banged up and has a concussion, but the doctor didn't think she needed to be hospitalized or anything."

"Your mom wouldn't have agreed to go with him to any hospital anyway. She and your dad are back at the ranch waiting for us," said Howard. "They got so frightened they were beside themselves when they heard that you were missing, so they wouldn't even consider going anywhere until you were found. Gail and I had quite a job trying to calm them down."

He turned again and clucked to the horse. I tried to take in what he had just said. Had my parents really been frightened for me? I couldn't quite picture it. They kept going places and leaving me behind as if I didn't mean more than the furniture in the house, and now they had supposedly gotten all on edge because I didn't come home? But why would Howard say it if it weren't true...?

I kept pondering the issue the whole way home, while Rigoletto carried me safely and surefooted through the forest. Even though he acted totally calm, I couldn't stop glancing nervously toward shrubs and bushes. What if the mountain lion was lurking in there, waiting for us to pass? But we saw no sign of it, and eventually, after what felt like a hundred years, we finally dismounted outside the paddock.

"You girls look completely wiped out," said Howard. "Go inside and get some more food first, and then it's off to bed with all three of you."

"Honestly Dad, you sound like we're three-year-olds or something," grumbled Suzanne. "But you're right. I'm so tired I could sleep forever."

"Hah, you're one to talk," I said teasingly, "You, who slept like a rock for hours last night." Then in the next moment I felt a knot in my stomach, from anxiety and anticipation. What would it be like to see my parents again? Had they really been as worried about me as Howard said? I would soon find out. I put my hand on the doorknob and pushed the door open.

Chapter 12

It was the day after. Lily and her dad had gone home, and Suzanne and I were standing in the paddock, grooming Rigoletto and Jasper.

We had groomed Silas first and were finished with him. He was now grazing peacefully, looking as though he didn't have a worry in the world, despite the fact that his right hind leg was bandaged. He'd be off duty for a week in order to let his wounds heal.

"You wouldn't think he'd been lost in the wilderness for several days," I said, pointing at him with the grooming brush. "Well, if you ignore the bandage, at least. It's pretty amazing that he got away with only a few minor cuts and bruises. He could just as easily have ended up as food for the wolves."

"Or gotten into the clutches of the mountain lion!" Suzanne made a face.

"I hope the rangers find the mountain lion soon and get it transported back to the reserve," I said hopefully. "I'd really love to see the bears again before I go home."

And I was hoping to take some pictures of them before we rolled rocks into the

opening. Suzanne, Lily and I had agreed to keep our discovery of the blue bears to ourselves. They had lived undisturbed in that valley for all these years. If the knowledge of them and the hidden valley got out, everything would be ruined. Scientists and tourists alike would inundate the place, and maybe even some trophy hunters who were willing to do just about anything to get their hands on a blue bearskin. Therefore we had decided to block the opening into the valley with rocks, so the bears wouldn't be able to come out that way. Every time one of them wandered off through the opening there was a higher risk of someone seeing them and finding the valley.

"Do you think it's such a good idea to take pictures, though?" Suzanne objected when I told her about my plan. "What if someone sees them?"

"Not to worry. I'm going to download them to my computer and save them in a secret folder. Then, some day, when my parents are old and gray and have quit going on expeditions... then I might just tell them what Lily discovered that time long, long ago."

Suzanne giggled. "Your dad will probably run after you and hit you with his cane! By the way, your mom looked a lot better this morning, don't you think?"

I nodded. "She said she felt much better, too, but she and my dad have still decided to stay for another week so that she can recover completely before we go home."

"I'm actually a little surprised that she let you out the door at all today, considering how hysterical she was when we came home yesterday," teased Suzanne. "And you thought your parents

didn't give a hoot about you. Were you wrong, or what?"

"If I hadn't seen it for myself, I wouldn't have believed it," I said. "They never seemed the slightest bit interested in me before, so I honestly didn't think they loved me very much." I smiled to myself. Now I knew that wasn't the case. But who would have thought that my mom, my daring and adventurous mom, had always been scared to death that something would happen to me?

"Your dad always thought we should take you along on our travels, ever since you were little," she had told me after having practically crushed me with hugs, and overwhelmed me with her worried questions. "You have no idea how often we argued about that particular issue! The thing is, I know how dangerous it can be in the places we go, and just the thought of taking a small, defenseless child into the unknown... No. It was better to know that you were safe and sound, back home with Grandma."

"But why didn't you ever tell me how you felt? Why did you let me think that you didn't care about me?" I looked accusingly at her.

Mom made a face and put her hands to her head. She probably has a terrible headache, I thought, feeling a pang of guilt for bugging her.

"I didn't know that you felt so unwanted... I honestly thought that those accusations that you threw at us before we went on this expedition were just something you said because you were so disappointed about our vacation going down the drain. I had no idea that you really meant it..."

Mom shook her head and made

another face. I probably ought to let her rest, but we couldn't stop now. This was too important.

"I'm utterly shocked that you actually believed that I don't care about you," she said as she took my hand. "That is as far from the truth as it could be. Yes, I know we have been gone a lot, but I really didn't think that you had a problem with it. You've always gotten along so well with Grandma, and I thought you understood why I didn't want to take you with us..." Mom's eyes were shiny, and she looked as though she were on the verge of tears.

"Why did you think that I understood it when you never told me?" I asked, noticing that I was near tears myself. "All the hurt feelings and difficult days I might have been spared, had I only known the truth earlier. I would have still missed you when you were gone, but at least I wouldn't have felt so unwanted and abandoned."

Mom stroked my hair and smiled gently. "Oh baby, I'm so sorry about all the misunderstandings. Both your dad and I have been unbelievably thoughtless and self-centered, I see that now. Do you think you can forgive us?"

Right then I couldn't say anything at all, but I think my teary smile was enough of an answer.

"I actually understand very well why my mom didn't dare take me along when I was little," I said a little later, glancing at my dad. He had kept silent while mom and I had been talking. "But in case you two haven't noticed, I'm not exactly a little kid anymore. I can take care of myself."

Dad started laughing. "You sure can! You've proven that much! Here we were, thinking we'd found a safe place for you to stay, and then as soon as we turned our backs, you went off into the wilderness and fought off mountain lions and wolves, and I don't know what all!"

"Well, I didn't exactly fight them off," I said, silently thinking that if Mom and Dad had seen me when we fled from that big, growling cat, they wouldn't have called me brave, that's for sure.

"The next time we go somewhere on an expedition, you'll definitely have to come," said Dad. "Your mom could use someone to protect her. She can't even sit on the lowest branch of a tree without causing a catastrophe!"

"How rude!" Mom laughed as she made a face at him. "I was at the very top of the tree, I'll have you know! But now my head is about to burst. I think I'd better try to sleep a little."

Dad and I walked quietly out of the room to let her get some rest. The most important things had been said. We could talk more later.

"I'm sorry your expedition didn't turn out the way you'd hoped," I said, and felt, to my surprise, that I meant it.

"Doesn't matter one bit," said Dad unconcerned. "There'll be other expeditions. The world is full of exciting places just waiting to be explored. What matters is that everyone came away reasonably unharmed from everything that happened. Besides, we didn't see a trace of the blue bears. The old hermit who lives up by the river almost died laughing when I told him what we'd heard. He's lived here his whole life and hasn't seen a single blue bear, so we felt rather silly, your mom and I, for having been fooled so easily. Oh well, we got some pretty nice pictures of some rare beavers, at least. Although a blue bear or two would, of course, have taken the cake. Too bad it was all lies, or somebody's vivid imagination."

I opened my mouth to say something, but closed it again.

"I think I'll go and lie down for a while too," I mumbled. "See you later, Dad."

My nap lasted most of the day, interrupted only by a hearty dinner. It was the first time I'd ever gone straight to bed from the dinner table. At first I felt like I could sleep for several days, but finally I was perky and rested again, although still somewhat stiff and sore from all the hard riding I'd done.

Maybe I should feel guiltier for not telling Dad about the blue bears, but a promise is a promise. And I thought the beautiful blue creatures deserved to live in peace in their little secret valley. It felt like the right thing to do, and I kind of liked the idea of sharing the secret with Suzanne and Lily.

I sighed contentedly as I pulled a brush across Rigoletto's back with long, slow strokes. He stood completely still and clearly enjoyed being groomed.

"Are you disappointed that you don't get to ride Silas?" asked Suzanne with a look at me.

I shook my head. "Rigoletto is more than good enough," I said, scratching him on the forehead. "He's so gentle, and nice to ride. The only problem is that he's a real chicken around mountain lions!"

Suzanne started laughing. "It's a good thing for you that he is," she said.

"Yes, thank goodness for that! Rigoletto is a real hero, aren't you, boy?"

He glanced at me with sleepy eyes, then snorted and started sniffing the ground, looking for something edible. Praise is good, but food is better, he seemed to think.

I smiled and scratched his mane. "You're sweet, Rigoletto!" I said. "Almost as sweet as Roofus." I noticed the familiar pang of longing for my own wonderful horse. But a week goes by pretty quickly. I'd be home soon, and back with Roofus. I was looking forward to it already. And man, did I have a lot of exciting stories to tell! I suddenly remembered the day when I stood under the tree, wishing that my parents would show that they loved me. So many scary things had happened afterwards, but my wish had come true. So who knows? Maybe the old moss-covered tree had some magic in it after all.